A Lifetime

of

Forever & Always

Mary E. Davis

With heartfelt thanks to Dona, Tom & Sarah

for sharing their mountain house and their friendship

with our family for many years!

Preface

Slowly, deftly, Daniel stroked her face, outlining its familiar curves, committing them to memory one final time. He took his time, lovingly tracing her features and soaking in the softness of her skin, knowing the memory would have to last for all eternity.

Still holding her face in his right hand, as Claire sat on the edge of the narrow bed, he took her left hand that she'd placed on his chest. They intertwined fingers, both of their eyes falling onto the simple gold wedding bands they'd exchanged over two decades earlier. Tears once again clouded their eyes, and then slowly, silently slid down their already tear-stained cheeks.

"I love you," Claire whispered, meaning it to the core of her soul.

Just as Daniel had done countless times before, he looked into her eyes, but his gaze reached deep into her heart.

"Forever," he answered.

Claire laid her head on Daniel's chest, leaning in to him, listening to the slow, rhythmic beat of his heart. Daniel held her tightly, breathing in the soft, familiar scent of her hair and silently closing his eyes.

Then suddenly, and all too soon, the offending, sickening squelch of the monitor next to the hospital bed filled the room with its evil sound and Daniel's grip loosened on Claire.

"No!" Claire screamed, "Daniel! *No!*"

She clutched him, lying across his chest sobbing and wailing as she desperately begged and pleaded for the only man she'd ever loved to come back to her.

A familiar nurse stepped quietly into the room, turning off the offensive monitor, and setting the other machines to continue circulating Daniel's blood so that his organs could be transplanted as he'd instructed.

Then she stepped closer to the bed and without a word, briefly laid her hand on Claire's back as it heaved with heartbroken sobs. Without a sound, she walked from the room, quietly closing the door behind her.

Chapter 1

After Daniel's death, Claire drifted robotically through her dreaded duties and obligations, making phone calls, notifying family and friends that her beloved Daniel was gone. Thankfully, several of her closest friends also shared the painful burden of letting others know that Daniel had passed away, which was a welcome relief to Claire.

Daniel hadn't wanted a traditional funeral wanting to spare Claire the agonizing casket selection and burial plot details. Months earlier, when it had become clear that his illness was worsening, Daniel had convinced Claire that they needed to talk about all those things that she had tried in earnest to avoid. Speaking of them meant that Claire would be facing a future without the man she'd loved for over half of her lifetime, a man whose touch made her whole world right, whose breath on her neck each night was a comforting reminder of the love and the life that they shared.

Daniel had insisted on making his own final arrangements in order to spare Claire the painful tasks. After finalizing his instructions with the crematorium, he told Claire that he'd prefer a 'Celebration of Life' in lieu of a traditional-style funeral. He'd explained to Claire that he wanted his family and friends to know how much he loved them and how much he loved his life and he wanted them to celebrate it after he was gone, rather than dwell on his passing.

During their years of marriage Daniel had always been 'the planner' in the family. It was he who took care of the details for everything from their finances to their family vacations. And Claire was the balancing force that was the creative one and the nurturer, making their house a home; taking care of their children's needs; the school activities; the social obligations and the holiday gatherings. It was obvious to all who knew them, that Claire and Daniel Mitchell each perfectly balanced the other, picking up where the other left off, and, at times, literally finishing each other's sentences. Their easy marriage had always been the envy of family and friends alike.

So Claire considered it to be in 'typical *Daniel* style' when he told her he'd made his own final arrangements, taking charge, as always. Yet she just couldn't bear to think of a life without him in it, let alone even picture herself as his grieving widow, speaking of him in the past tense.

Twenty-four years of marriage simply had not been enough for her. In years past, each time Daniel had said he'd love her 'forever,' Claire had always felt warm and secure, knowing they'd be together and in love till the end of time. Who knew that Daniel's illness would creep into their life and rob them of their 'forever?'

* * *

"No! Stop it! Enough!" she had screamed, putting up her hands, as Daniel methodically went over the details of how he thought Claire should deal with their finances and investments when he was gone. Propped on two overstuffed bed pillows on the leather sofa in their family room, Daniel leaned forward and gently pulled Claire to him, holding her as she sobbed inconsolably.

"If not for the kids, I *swear* I don't think I'd even want to *be* here without you, Daniel!" Claire said, honestly preferring to leave the Earth when he did, rather than live with the painful heartache that she knew lay ahead of her.

"But, I know Danny and Layne will need me more than ever if you're not here," she added.

"And **you** still have a whole life ahead of you, too, Claire," Daniel told her, stroking her shiny, auburn hair as she buried her wet face against him and cried into his chest.

He held her till she finally quieted again and drew in a deep, spastic breath, and then exhaled slowly.

"I'll be okay. I will," she said, sitting upright, "But after we finish talking about all these plans you've made for me, I don't ever want to speak of the subject again!"

Nodding his agreement, Daniel went on, reminding Claire of his sizable life insurance policies; the 'Buy-Sell Agreement' he'd had drawn up years earlier with his business partner; their various stocks and annuities; several income-producing rental properties that they owned and the trust he'd formed and funded years earlier.

"So, really, Claire, you're going to be in great financial-shape!" Daniel said, "No worries at all!"

"Daniel, I'd rather be living in a cardboard box, under a bridge with **you**, than have all the money in the **world**," she said sadly, meaning every word.

"I know," he added, "But at least I'll know that you and the kids are going to be okay," he said with relief in his tired voice.

"Oh," he added, "And just one more thing, Hon! Don't forget, when the time comes, that I'm an organ donor. And I've already signed all the paperwork with Dr. March, so things are already set-up."

"Okay, got it," Claire said, scooping up all the loose papers and file folders that were scattered on the nearby coffee table and on the floor beside the sofa.

"And now, Mr. Mitchell, if we're finished with all this morbid, depressing stuff, I'll go make us some dinner!"

Chapter 2

Shortly after Daniel's death, Claire found herself constantly drifting back to sweet memories of simpler, more carefree, times.

The shrill whistle blew on the teakettle and Claire was jarred back into her cruel, biting reality. Reaching for the steaming red kettle, she desperately wished she were making two cups of tea, not one.

She was aware of the biting reality that the second half of her life was going to be about singular, solitary and lonely things in her new 'Life of One.' One place setting on the table; one pair of shoes by the door; one side of the bed to make each morning; one toothbrush by the sink; one set of car keys on the counter; a lonely never-ending life of 'ones.' How could she possibly face it all without Daniel?

Pouring the steaming water into her mug, Claire heard the door to the laundry room open.

"Mom?" she heard her son's deep voice call out. "We're here!" his voice getting closer as he dropped his heavy duffel bag on the wood floor in the family room.

Danny and his sister Layne went straight to Claire, hugging her close. The three remaining Mitchells all dissolved into loud, heavy sobs, clutching each other as they cried for the man they'd all loved so.

"Mom, was he in pain?" Layne asked through her sobs.

"No, Honey," Claire said, "Not at all."

"What about you, Mom?" Danny asked, "How are you doing?"

"I'm just so glad you guys are here," Claire said, avoiding Danny's question as best she could.

Later that afternoon, Claire sat with Danny and Layne in their family room. She was curled up on the sofa with her bare feet under her. Layne way stretched out on the sofa with her head in her mom's lap as Claire ran her fingers through her daughter's long, soft hair. Danny was in one of the oversized recliners across the room. In happier times, it was a scene played out over and over in the Mitchell home. Daniel and Danny would be stretched out in the two, big recliners watching a ballgame on TV. And Claire and Layne would be on the sofa, with Claire reading and Layne dozing beside her mom, just happy to have a break from her hectic college schedule.

But this was no happy, family time, as Claire and the kids sat quietly, listening to the rain patter outside. Watching the raindrops bounce off the pool water's surface outside, Danny said, "Mom, I'm sorry I wasn't here."

"Oh, Danny, you know your dad wanted you guys to stick to your exam schedules. He was thrilled you were here last weekend! And, besides, we had no idea when the end would come!"

"I know, Mom, but we wanted to be here for *you*, too," Layne added, "You were all alone!"

"No! I didn't feel alone at all, Honey," Claire said reassuringly. "Daddy was with me! And he wanted you both to know how much he loved you! We're all gonna be okay. I promise!" She leaned down and kissed the top of Layne's head, tears forming in her eyes, but her heart full of love for her children.

The next morning, Claire slowly opened her eyes. She lay perfectly still on her right side, not wanting to move, willing herself to still feel Daniel beside her. She knew if she rolled over that her nightmare would be real and she'd be alone in their big bed. She closed her eyes again, shutting out reality and trying to feel Daniel beside her still. But she felt so alone.

Suddenly, a knock at the door mercifully reminded her that she wasn't alone in the house.

"Morning, Mom," Layne said opening the bedroom door and carrying a mug of hot coffee for Claire.

"Oh! What time is it?" Claire asked, feeling like she should be in the kitchen making breakfast for her kids.

"Nearly ten," Layne told her, "We thought you needed some sleep. You've been sleeping in a hospital chair for over two weeks."

'*The hospital*' Claire thought, instantly wishing she could be back in that hospital room with Daniel again, cloistered away from the world, from her harsh new reality.

"Mom, the family will start arriving today," Layne reminded Claire as she sat up on the edge of her bed so she could sip her coffee.

"Right," Claire said, dreading the influx of people and the pomp and circumstance that would surely follow.

"Well, Danny and I have made-up the guest bedrooms already," Layne said, as she silently collected used tissues from the nearby night table, realizing her mom must have cried herself to sleep.

"Oh, you guys are great!" Claire said, appreciating her kind children all the more, and adding, "I've got to go by the funeral home today to handle a few things." She didn't want to tell her nineteen-year old daughter that she had to go and pick-up her dad's ashes.

"Do you want me or Danny to come with you?" Layne offered.

"No," Claire told her, "Why don't you and Danny stay here and wait for MeMa and all the family to get here?" referring to her own mother and her in-laws. Claire's dad had died years earlier and Daniel's parents had been killed in a car accident when he was in college.

Daniel's two older brothers and their families were flying in to the Orlando airport. And Claire's younger sister, Eva, was catching a flight later that day out of New York, where she worked as an assistant to a well-known fashion designer. Although close as children, Eva and Claire had grown apart over the years after Claire had settled down and started a family and Eva had chosen a more jet-set lifestyle.

Layne left her mom alone so she could get dressed for her day. Claire slid from her bed, not wanting to face the day ahead. She walked into her large, marble-tiled bathroom and absent-mindedly turned on the wall switch for the ceiling stereo speakers as she had done for years, before she showered.

Minutes later, standing in the shower, with the hot water rhythmically pelting down on her back, Claire's gaze fell to Daniel's razor, propped in the shower niche, never to shave his handsome face again. She remembered that she'd offered to bring it to the hospital for him, but he'd asked her to simply bring him a few disposable razors instead. Looking at the heavy, silver metal razor now, the tears instantly began to flow and Claire was sobbing once again. She leaned against the beige marbled shower wall and slid down it sitting on the floor, drawing her knees to her chest, and hysterically sobbing.

Her body was convulsing in uncontrolled sobs as the water beat down on her crouched figure.

"God! Why?" she screamed "Why did you take him from me?"

Her head in her hands, as the water swirled down the drain in the floor below her, Claire realized that the song that played overhead was the song she and Daniel had danced to at their wedding. She stifled her sobs, straining to hear the lyrics over the sound of the water.

"*Always and forever – these moments with you – "* it went on and on as Claire willed herself to quiet her cries, remembering how many times she and Daniel had listened to what Daniel had dubbed 'their song.' He'd asked the band to play it one night when they were at their anniversary dinner so he and Claire could dance barefoot in the sand at the beachside restaurant after dinner; he'd once dedicated it to her on a radio call-in show when they were in college; he'd even attempted to sing it to her once at a karaoke bar, which was especially sweet, although he took a lot of ribbing from his friends for it.

Claire closed her eyes, listening to 'their song,' letting the lyrics wash over her.

By the time it ended, she felt strong enough to stand up and finish her shower.

An hour later, composed once again, and dressed in a classic taupe-colored sweater set and tailored black slacks, Claire walked into her kitchen, unseen by her children.

Danny and Layne were at the kitchen table laughing as they looked through a family photo album with their backs to her.

"Look!" Layne said, "Here's Dad pushing the boat off that sandbar in the Keys!"

"Yep!" Danny said, raising an eyebrow at his little sister, "After you ran us aground, as I recall!"

As Claire watched her handsome grown children, with their dad's good looks and witty charm, she knew she had to be strong for them. They deserved to have at least one parent. But she also desperately longed for Daniel to be back with them again.

"Oh, hey, Mom!" Danny said looking up.

"Morning," Claire said, "But then it's nearly noon, isn't it?! I *really* overslept!"

Layne got up to place her empty mug in the sink.

"Mom, how 'bout something to eat?"

"No, thanks," Claire answered, "I'm going to run over to the funeral home and take care of things now."

"Mom, wait a sec! Let me drive you," Danny said jumping up from the table with his empty plate.

"No, no, I'm fine, Honey," Claire said, "Really! I won't be long."

Chapter 3

Claire went to her Volvo and opened it's driver's door, then slowly closed it, still standing by her car, looking across it's roof, at the other vehicle parked in her garage. After a few seconds, she went round to the driver's side of Daniel's SUV. She'd never liked to drive it before, always saying it was too big for her to park.

But, today, she wanted nothing more than to be inside the big, silver Armada that always faintly smelled of Daniel's cologne. Opening the door, Claire was immediately awash with the familiar smell of Daniel's signature Polo scent that she'd so loved over the years.

She stepped onto the shiny running board and up into the leather driver's seat. Too far away from the steering wheel and pedals, she instinctively reached for the electric lever to adjust the seat. Beginning to move it forward, she stopped abruptly.

'Oh, God!' she thought, 'I'll never have to move his seat again!' realizing Daniel would never drive his car again. Never. Ever. She closed her eyes to steady herself as she felt her chest tightening again.

Inhaling deeply, she tried desperately to fill her self with Daniel's sweet, yet manly, scent and hoping somehow to fill the cavernous hole within her heart.

Moments later, she closed the car's door, buckled her seatbelt, adjusted the car's mirrors and then carefully backed out of the garage, enveloped in the familiar scent of Daniel. Reaching down to slide the car's gearshift into 'drive,' Claire caught sight of Daniel's oversized sunglasses. They were right where he'd left them the last time he'd driven his car. They sat, waiting for Daniel to come back and slip them on once again, as he'd done more than a thousand times before.

Claire slowly put on his large sunglasses, as if to bring Daniel a bit closer to her in some way, and she continued on the short drive to the funeral home.

Only a few minutes later, she pulled the SUV under the tall covered portico of the funeral home. Claire felt a bit dizzy and lightheaded as she switched off the car's engine.

"You can do this," she said aloud, still not believing she was about to pick up the ashes of her beloved Daniel.

Entering the huge, heavy double-door entry, Claire was immediately greeted by a smartly dressed man who extended his hand in greeting.

"Ah, yes, Mrs. Mitchell! We've been expecting you. I'm William Ayers, director of the funeral home."

Suddenly aware of the huge sunglasses she was still wearing, Claire took them off quickly, and shook his hand.

"Very nice to meet you, Mr. Ayers," she said awkwardly.

"And now if you'll follow me, Mrs. Mitchell, I'll take you to our Memory Gardens, where your husband is waiting," Mr. Ayers said.

'*Odd choice of words*,' Claire thought, wishing Daniel would jump up to greet her when she walked in to the garden.

Claire was led down a long carpeted corridor, past a small chapel and a couple of quiet offices. Turning right, she saw a set of glass doors beyond which were several benches beside a small fountain surrounded by lush greenery.

"Right this way, please," Mr. Ayers gestured as he held a door open for Claire.

Claire walked hesitantly in to the garden area. Her eyes immediately fixed on the simple white box tied with twine sitting atop a lone pedestal table. Although she knew the box contained Daniel's ashes, she thought it looked more like a take-out box or a box from her local bakery.

"Please, sit," Mr. Ayers said, gesturing toward the bench nearest Claire. As Claire took a seat beside the white box, Mr. Ayers pulled an envelope from inside a pocket of his suit jacket. Claire assumed it was simply a copy of the forms that Daniel had signed months earlier when he'd made arrangements for his cremation.

"Mrs. Mitchell, this is for you," he began. "Your husband asked that I personally give it to you when we met. I'll leave you alone now. Please take all the time you need."

And with that, Mr. Ayers touched Claire's shoulder briefly, and then turned to leave her alone in the gardens.

Still assuming that the envelope held a copy of a form or maybe even another one of Daniel's many instructional notes, Claire ripped open the envelope. Glancing toward the white box that held the remains of her love, she unfolded the white, heavy-stock paper that she recognized was Daniel's firm's letterhead. Immediately she recognized the familiar handwriting.

Taking a deep breath, Claire read:

Claire, My Love~

If you are reading this now, I know this is a difficult time for you – for all of you, really. I'm so, so sorry to leave you all, Claire. But, I know you'll all be fine and that you'll get through this. You're the strongest person I've ever known

~ and I know your strength is going to help Layne and Danny now too. I really hope they'll get back to their classes in Gainesville quickly. They know I want them to finish school and get on with their goals just as they'd planned. I'll be there with you the day they both graduate, Claire ~ right there beside you, just like we'd always planned.

Now, Claire, as we talked about months ago, I want you to go on with your life. Don't ever stop living. Don't ever stop loving. You have so much left to do. So much left to share with the world. Just know that whatever you do and wherever you go, I'm right there beside you, just like always. You're such a beautiful woman, Claire ~ more beautiful than that first day I saw you on campus ~ In all my life, I'd never liked the Gators, till I met you! And I shocked everyone, including myself, when I transferred to Gainesville just to be near you! Only YOU could have made me do that!

Claire stopped reading his note, took a deep breath, closed her eyes and remembered that spectacular fall day when she'd first laid eyes on Daniel. She couldn't help but smile as she remembered.

*

She had been a freshman at the University of Florida and had been rushing across the massive, oak-shaded Gainesville campus, juggling a stack of books and a Grande-sized latte' intent on getting to class on time.

All of a sudden, she saw a gorgeous, dark-haired man, who was chatting with a couple guys, old friends it turned out, who he'd come to visit on the campus.

Claire literally stopped dead in her tracks, mesmerized by the tall, handsome, muscular guy just twenty feet away.

She was certain, in that instant, that she'd never laid eyes on a better-looking man in all her life. Not caring who saw her, she took inventory of the gorgeous young man who was laughing and talking with his friends, his hands casually tucked into his jeans' front pockets.

She was at once captivated by Daniel's perfect smile; his thick, brown hair, just touching the collar of his shirt in back; his deep tan; and the well-defined biceps that she could even see through his shirt's sleeves.

As if he'd felt her stare, Daniel looked toward Claire with his brilliant emerald green eyes and flashed that huge, white grin at her. Embarrassed and flustered that he'd caught her staring, Claire briefly smiled, and then rushed past Daniel and his friends, arriving late to her class and red-faced.

Claire would find out later that Daniel had skipped his own classes at a different university and had gone to the exact same spot, at the exact, same time every day for the next week, just hoping to see her again on the huge campus!

Finally, after a week, Claire had the same class again, and was once again rushing to the giant lecture hall. Looking down, she was studying notes for an exam.

As Daniel stepped toward her, Claire literally walked right into him, at once, dropping her books.

"I'm so sorry!" he said, somewhat embarrassed and quickly stooping to retrieve her books.

Claire quickly squatted down, collecting her binders and books and their eyes met. The world around her stood still as she looked into the most intense green eyes she'd ever seen.

Daniel's mouth went dry and he was instantly overwhelmed by the striking vision in front of him. Claire's shiny auburn hair hung loosely past her shoulders and her perfect, tanned skin with its delicate, almost angelic features was more perfect than anything he'd ever seen.

Neither could speak as they looked into each other's eyes barely breathing for a few seconds. Then, Daniel swallowed hard, cleared his throat and somehow clumsily found his voice again.

"I'm so sorry! I didn't mean to startle you," he said, flashing his perfect, game show host grin again. "My name is Dan Mitchell."

Awkwardly, Claire said, "I'm Claire ~ Um, Claire Douglas."

Both still crouched, Daniel extended his tanned hand to Claire. She took it, shaking hands with the incredibly handsome young man. Then, Daniel placed his left hand under Claire's right elbow and helped her to stand up as he continued to look into her eyes.

Once again, the stack of books fell off the top of her knees and onto the ground, this time unnoticed by either Claire or Daniel.

Still holding her hand, the drop-dead gorgeous man said, "Well, Claire, it's great to finally meet you! I know you have a class now, but I was hoping we could possibly get a bite to eat later… If you're free, that is."

Stammering and not wanting to release his strong, tanned hand, Claire said, "Uh, yeah! That would be great. Could we meet somewhere?"

"My buddies say Eduardo's is good. How about 8:00 then?" Daniel suggested, trying to mask his gushing enthusiasm.

And with that, he dared to lightly kiss the back of Claire's hand that he was still holding, and then he reluctantly released it. Claire was certain she'd faint at that very moment.

Daniel collected her books for her yet again and handed the stack to her, grinning that fabulous grin. "See you tonight, Claire Douglas! I'll be counting the minutes!" he said as he winked at her and walked away leaving Claire speechless

but with her heart racing as she watched
his jeans till they were out of her sight.

*

Opening her eyes, Claire realized
that tears had been running down her face
and onto her neck, spilling onto her
sweater top. She reached for a nearby
Kleenex and dabbed her eyes, then resumed
reading Daniel's letter.

*

Claire, we had 26 years together in all ~ 24 of them married ~ and we did more living in those years than most people do in a lifetime. Two phenomenal kids, who have become such awesome adults. (Who, thankfully, got your good looks!) A love that few people are lucky enough to ever find. Careers that we've both loved. Our dream house that you turned into a home for our family. More travels and good times than we'd ever dreamed possible. Because of you, Claire, I had such a rich life! Full of more love than I could have ever hoped for! I'm glad we got to talk, Claire ~ really talk about things. You know I want you get on with your life. Don't waste a day of it! You're only 45 and you are so beautiful, smart and vibrant. You deserve to be happy and to always be loved. Please find love once again, Claire, so you're not alone for a minute! And, remember, my love, it won't mean that our love will ever end.

I'm with you always, loving you forever,

Daniel

Claire exhaled, leaning her head back to look up at the clear, blue sky. Warm, wet tears streaked her face, as she clutched Daniel's letter to her chest.

Minutes later, she collected herself, neatly folded Daniel's letter again and replaced it in it's envelope.

As she stood up, Claire stared hesitantly at the white box waiting for her on the pedestal table. She knew she wouldn't open the box. She reached for it tentatively as her hands trembled.

Picking it up, she was surprised that such a small box could hold her six-foot tall, broad-shouldered husband. She hugged it to her stomach tightly.

"Oh, Daniel," she spoke aloud, but in a whisper, "I miss you so much!"

Turning, she carefully carried the remains of her love as if the white box were priceless crystal. She found Mr. Ayers waiting for her in the reception area inside. He walked toward her and asked if there was anything he could do for her.

"No, Mr. Ayers, but thank you for all your help," Claire told him.

"Well, we've had some inquiries about the arrangements for your husband's service," he told her, "And we've passed on the information about Mr. Mitchell's

'Celebration of Life' service at your home tomorrow, just as you've asked."

"Thank you," Claire said, "I appreciate all your help."

And with that, Claire carried the box outside, as Mr. Ayers held the front door open for her. It all seemed so surreal to her.

Stepping up into the big SUV, Claire realized she didn't know what to do with the white box. She'd never held the ashes of anyone, lest of all, someone as important to her as her precious Daniel.

As she sat in the driver's seat, she first bent forward and then to her right, to place the box on the floor mat in front of the passenger's seat.

'No, that just doesn't seem right,' she silently thought to herself.

She next sat the box beside her on the leather passenger's seat and then buckled her own seatbelt. Looking to her right, she quickly reached over, pulled the seatbelt forward and buckled the passenger seatbelt around the white box.

She then put on Daniel's big sunglasses and pulled the SUV onto the highway.

Chapter 4

As Claire turned the SUV around the corner and onto her tree-lined street, she saw about ten cars parked in her driveway and on the street.

"God," she prayed aloud, "Help me to get through all this!" She'd been dreading the houseful of well-meaning and good-intentioned family and friends that awaited her.

She pulled into her garage, parking next to her white Volvo, and shut off the car's engine. Stepping down from the SUV, she left the white box on the front seat still strapped in, thinking she'd prepare Danny and Layne first, before bringing it into the house.

Walking inside, Claire was met by her mother, whom Danny had dubbed MeMa when he was just a young toddler.

"Claire," she said, rushing to hug her daughter.

"Hi, Mom," Claire said, realizing that she was genuinely glad her mother was there.

Both women hugged tightly as they instantly dissolved into sobs, needing no further words between them.

After what had seemed like *forever*, they released one another, each dabbing their eyes with Kleenex they'd pulled from their own pockets.

"Come on, Honey," Jill Douglas said to her daughter as she took Claire's hand and led her into the kitchen where Daniel's brothers and their families were gathered round the table and at the bar top at the end of Claire's kitchen.

Seeing Claire, they all got up to greet her and Claire could see they'd all been crying. Jon, Daniel's oldest brother, hugged Claire first.

"Claire, how're you holding up?" he asked.

"Better than I'd expected honestly," she said, as she next turned to Mark, the middle brother in Daniel's family.

"Hey, Mark," she said hugging him.

"Claire," he said, "God, I just can't believe it."

"I know," she said honestly.

Then Jon's wife, Sarah; and Mark's wife, Kellie; came up and also greeted Claire, both genuinely sad to lose Dan, whom they'd both loved like a brother over the years.

"If there's anything you need," Kellie offered.

"I know," Claire said, "Thanks."

Then, suddenly interrupting the somber moment, the kitchen door slammed shut as Jon's and Sarah's seven-year old twins, Amanda and Alex, ran through

Claire's kitchen, screaming and waving sticks.

Claire called out behind them, "Uh, hi, girls!" as the *Terrible Twins*, as Daniel had affectionately dubbed them, tore through the group as the adults instinctively parted a path for them. Close on the girls' heels, Layne was right behind them, trying to confiscate the sticks they were wielding in the house. She shot her mom a desperate look, rolling her eyes, as she ran past her.

The chaos continued as Danny ran down the stairs following Mark and Kellie's three kids, each under the age of ten.

Claire was relieved when she caught sight of her best friend, Elaine, who was coming into the kitchen to hang up the cordless phone on the desk.

"Hi, Hon," Elaine said, "That was your neighbor, Joan. She said she'd be by later with a casserole."

Rolling her eyes, Claire said, "Yeah, we're really starving over here," she said, looking past Elaine's and at the dozens of casserole dishes and covered desserts that people had already brought by the house earlier in the day.

"Oh, Claire," Elaine said, "Hope it's okay, but Ryan is on Daniel's computer right now and is working on the video montage for the service tomorrow."

"Of course! Yes!" Claire said, "And thank you!"

Walking through the dining room, Claire found Jim Taylor and his wife, Leesa, arranging dozens of plants and floral baskets on the table and sideboard. Jim had been Daniel's oldest friend. They'd been buddies since high school, had played football together for years and were as close as brothers.

Claire hugged Leesa first, and then Jim.

"Thanks for coming, guys," she told them both.

"You're family, Claire," Jim told her, "You know that."

Just then, a group of college friends of Layne and Danny came up to Claire to hug her, all politely paying their respects. Claire saw that most of them, even the guys, had been crying.

As Claire greeted the houseful of people, she was silently preoccupied with Daniel's ashes, still strapped in the front seat of the SUV in the garage. She'd wanted to talk with Layne and Danny first, before bringing the box callously into the house without warning.

Claire walked back in to the kitchen where Kellie handed her a glass of iced tea.

"Thanks," Claire said, rubbing her forehead, "I really need to find some aspirin!"

Suddenly, little Alex burst into the room.

"Aunt Claire! Aunt Claire! You forgot this cake in your car!" she said.

"Can we have some, pleeeez?!" Katie squealed, right on her sister's heels.

"Oh, no!" Claire said, all eyes on her now, as Layne and Danny came into the kitchen from different directions, unaware of what was happening.

Composing herself, Claire answered Katie, if only to stop the incessant begging!

"Uh, no, Honey. No cake now. Maybe later."

Kellie took the little white box, unknowingly from the rambunctious child, and placed it on the counter next to the ever-mounting collection of casseroles and desserts that had been dropped off at the Mitchell home.

"But, but…." Claire had tried to protest, as Layne guided her mom's shoulders, leading her from the kitchen and toward her bedroom.

"Mom, come lie down," she insisted, "Aunt Kellie said you need some aspirin. I'll get the bottle for you. Come on now. It's quiet in here!"

As Layne turned back her mom's thick comforter, she said, "Mom, you really need some rest now! We'll see if we can corral the monsters out there. Danny mentioned spiking their Kool-Aid with Benadryl!"

With her head pounding, Claire was feeling too exhausted to argue with her suddenly very grown-up daughter. She gratefully lay down on her pillow and closed her eyes.

Hours later, Claire awakened in a dark, quiet room and noticed her headache was gone. She got up and walked to the tiled area between the two separate walk-in closets just off her bedroom.

Hesitating, she reached for the handle to Daniel's closet. Slowly, she opened it, closing her eyes and immediately inhaling Daniel's familiar scent once again. He'd always kept his colognes on the built-in valet in his closet, so she had always said his closet 'smelled like Daniel.'

Claire stepped inside and stiffly sat down on the thick cream-colored plush carpet. Drawing her knees upward to her chin, she wrapped her arms round her legs as she looked around the big closet.

Daniel's slacks all hung neatly on the hangers from the dry cleaner; his pressed shirts hung, waiting for him to select one for the day; his sweaters sat neatly folded on their shelf; leather belts hung in their place and tailored suit jackets waited to hang across Daniel's broad shoulders once again.

But she knew that Daniel would never wear any of it *ever* again. Never touch anything in his closet *ever* again. Including Claire, she realized. He'd never touch *Claire* again. Tears filled her eyes once more as her chest tightened.

Minutes later, Claire heard her daughter come in to her room.

"Mom?" she heard Layne call out as she walked closer to the open closet door.

"Uh, Mom? *What* are you doing?" Layne said, looking down at her mom sitting cross-legged now on the floor of her father's closet.

"Oh, Honey," Claire said, dissolving in sobs, her head in her hands. Layne went to her mom and knelt down, hugging her tightly and rocking her slowly.

"It's gonna be okay, Mom. It will! It has to be!"

Danny appeared in the doorway of the closet. They heard his voice before they saw him as he walked closer.

"Well, the last of them has gone and Me-Ma has taken the family to uh - what are you two doing?" he said, looking down at Claire and Layne.

"Today was a hard day," Claire tried to explain, "I'd been dreading it! And then all the people…. I had to pick-up your dad's - his - uh- the white box!"

"No! Mom!" Danny said, his eyes widening in disbelief as he remembered his little cousin excitedly carrying the box and asking for a piece of cake.

"Oh my… ! No *way*!" Layne said, as realization flashed across her face too.

Then, they all looked at each other and immediately burst out laughing and crying at the same time, as they remembered the earlier scene in the kitchen with the *Terrible Twins* and what the children had **thought** was a bakery box.

"Um," Danny spoke first, "Does that mean Dad is still sitting between a chicken casserole and a chocolate cake on the kitchen counter?"

"Possibly so," Claire said, and they all laughed again, realizing that Daniel would have gotten the biggest kick of all out of the entire scene.

"Dad would have loved this story!" Danny said.

"Oh, yeah!" Claire said, knowing Danny was absolutely right. "Well, I *had* wanted to break it to you gently that I'd picked up his ashes," Claire said.

"And **that** you did, Mom!" Danny said, always appreciating his family's sense of humor.

Chapter 5

The next morning, the Mitchell house awakened early. MeMa had her five youngest grandkids outside on the dock at the river. She was keeping a close eye on them all as they cast their lines in hopes of catching a redfish although she really wasn't certain if it was the right time of the year for redfish.

Dan had always been the fisherman in the family. Their Uncle Dan had taught all of the kids to fish and they all loved to come to Florida to visit him. Daniel always took time out of his busy schedule to spend time with his nieces and nephews, often taking them fishing on his boat or teaching them to water ski on the river, just like he'd done with his own children. Claire had often joked that Daniel was really just an overgrown kid in an adult's body and all the children adored their favorite uncle.

Waking up slowly, Claire was grateful to her mom that the house was so peaceful and quiet. Her mother always seemed to know just what Claire needed.

Putting on her cozy pink, chenille robe, Claire's gaze fell to the framed photo of Daniel and herself that she kept on her dresser. It was an informal snapshot, taken in the mountains of Virginia a couple years earlier. Daniel had actually snapped the photo himself, holding the camera as both he and Claire looked into its lens. Just before he'd snapped the photo, he'd surprised Claire by kissing her cheek, making her laugh.

Looking at the photo now, Claire was truly dreading the day ahead of her. She felt like it was all a bad dream.

Could it be possible that she was now Daniel's *widow*?

'What a horrible word – 'widow,' she thought to herself. The finality of it all seemed so cruel. Such a lonely, dark, cold word, Claire thought.

Knowing the guests would start arriving at her house in just a few hours, Claire realized she'd have to pull herself together. Walking into her kitchen in her bare feet, she found some of the family around her kitchen table.

"Good Morning!" Kellie said, trying to sound cheerful, as she placed a dish in the sink, "Feel like something to eat?"

"No, thanks," Claire said, "I'll just get a cup of tea, I think."

Then, looking past the table, through the bank of kitchen windows, she saw her handsome, shirtless son on Daniel's riding lawnmower in the backyard. Behind Claire, Layne came into the kitchen carrying a basket of neatly folded laundry.

"Good grief!" Claire said, "Looks like the troops have been at it for hours! You guys are amazing!"

"Everybody just wants to give you a hand today," Kellie told her, "Your kids were up before dawn! They're really something, Claire!"

"I really don't know what I'd do without those two!" Claire said shaking her head as she looked out the window at her handsome son who looked so much like his father had looked when Claire had first met Daniel.

After leaving the clothesbasket at the foot of the stairs, Layne came back into the kitchen and gave her mom a kiss. "Sleep well, Mom?"

"Actually, I think I did," Claire said.

"Well, Danny put Dad's 'box' in the big cabinet in his office and he said he'd move it to Dad's closet when you woke up, so don't worry about it!" Layne told her mom.

"Yeah, Claire," Jon added from the end of the kitchen, "The kids shared the 'box story' with us! I had no idea!"

"Oh, Claire!" Sarah added, "I'm so sorry! Our girls are a bit, um, *spirited*, at times. I'm really sorry though!"

"Don't worry about it, Sarah!" Claire told her in complete honestly. "We really needed the levity around here! And Daniel would have gotten a kick out of it!"

Just before 2:00, the guests began to arrive. There were friends of Daniel's; friends of Claire's; dozens of neighbors; relatives from both sides who'd come from all over the country; lots of friends of Danny's and Layne's; Daniel's employees from his architectural firm; business associates of both Claire and Daniel and even some of Daniel's business *competitors* who had come to honor the man who they all had loved and respected over the years.

Fortunately, most of the neighbors had offered their driveways for additional parking and there was a nearby community park that accommodated all the overflow parking. Some of Danny's friends had organized an impromptu shuttle service to drive people from the park up to the house, which was a welcome convenience, especially for some of the older guests.

Claire was dressed in a silk navy dress with three-quarter sleeves and the pearls Daniel had given her on their last anniversary. She tried to greet each person as they arrived. Everyone mingled throughout the downstairs of the large, comfortable Mitchell home, remarking on what an incredible job Dan had done with the renovations of the old historic home.

During the renovation process on the rambling home, Daniel had specifically designed the open floor plan so it would be more conducive to entertaining. The downstairs consisted of an ample living room with tall ceilings and beautiful woodwork; a formal dining room; a sound-insulated media room with seating for ten; a tremendous gourmet kitchen; Daniel's office; Claire's office; two bedrooms; and a huge family room that also opened on to a large screened patio with a pool.

Sadly, when Daniel had re-designed the house, he could have never known that it would one day accommodate the hundreds of people who'd come to pay their respects to him and his family on that sad day.

Layne and Danny had set-up photo displays in almost every room as a sort-of memorial to their dad. There were various photos of Daniel everywhere throughout the house. Some were framed on tables and Layne had created large collages of family photos that she displayed on several easels.

There were lots of pictures of Daniel with his prized catches of various fish; one of Daniel with Danny after a Little League game; one with Layne at the sixth grade Father-Daughter dance; and on a family vacation in the Bahamas; skiing in Lake Tahoe; diving in the Caribbean; hiking in the mountains and just playfully mugging for the camera. Each photo held a special significance and Layne had alternately laughed and cried as she'd created the collages as a tribute to her dad, wanting to share his life with all their family and friends one last time.

People congregated around the photos and Claire could hear non-stop snippets of comments like "Great guy!" or "Best father!" and "Never met a stranger!"

Claire's head was beginning to feel woozy just as she felt a hand on her arm.

"Claire," Ryan, Elaine's husband said, "Are you ready to start?"

"Ah, sure," Claire answered hesitantly, drawing in a jagged breath.

Ryan went through the house asking everyone to meet in the family room to view the commemorative video he'd created.

Literally with standing-room-only, the guests in the family room overflowed onto the attached patio area, as everyone craned their necks to see the gigantic TV screen in the family room.

As the music began, the screen vividly came to life and read

"*Daniel James Mitchell 1961 – 2008.*"

Claire was sitting on the sofa near the huge screen beside Elaine, her own mom, and her sister, Eva. She drew in a deep breath, readying herself to see Daniel's image, as big as life in front of her.

Layne was nearby on an oversized ottoman and Danny was sitting on the floor at her feet, eager to see his full-of-life dad on the screen. With the music playing in the background, Ryan had started the video with Daniel's black-and-white baby photo; then added photos showing him with his older brothers.

There were dozens of photos that Claire had never seen before that Ryan had obviously borrowed from Daniel's brothers for use in the video. As the screen moved, there was little Daniel missing his first tooth; sitting at his desk in school; playing youth football; with a broken arm as a young boy; proudly standing by his first car, a red Camaro that he'd loved and holding up his acceptance letter to Florida State. And then, there he was with his arm around a young, beautiful Claire, both of them looking at each other, rather than into the camera. Claire reached for a Kleenex as Elaine put a hand on her shoulder for support and Danny went to stand behind his mom, putting his hand, reassuringly, on her other shoulder.

Ryan had done an incredible job on the video. It had been his gift to the Mitchells. The tribute continued with photos of Daniel and Claire at their simple, outdoor garden wedding, and it continued with photos of them moving into their tiny apartment in Gainesville, so Claire could finish college, after Daniel had already graduated. Then there was Daniel in front of their fixer-upper home they'd bought on the river so many years before. And then there was a young Daniel with Claire proudly holding Danny only moments after he was born.

The photos rolled on, till there literally wasn't a dry eye in the house, and Claire swore her heart would burst. Everyone watched as the video continued and Daniel's life began to come full circle. Layne, the proverbial 'Daddy's Girl' was born. Daniel stood proudly in front of the office building he'd bought to house his architectural firm. Then there were photos of birthday parties; Christmas mornings; and Daniel and Claire standing proudly with the kids in their caps and gowns at their high school graduations.

Then, suddenly, the music changed as the photos kept rolling, and everyone heard *"Always & Forever... these moments with you... "* And Claire swore that, just for a moment, it was Daniel's hand on her shoulders, not Danny's, that was comforting her, giving her strength.

As soon as the video tribute ended, Claire stood up, feeling strong once again, as she wiped away tears from her swollen eyes.

"I want to thank you all for being so good to Daniel and to our family," she began, "His life was so full because each all of you was in it. He said so many times that he was rich, not because of money or possessions, but thanks to the love of his family and his friends."

When Claire had finished speaking, Ryan stood up, wiping away his own tears, and told the teary-eyed group that they were welcome to share a few words about Dan, too.

Without hesitation, Danny immediately walked to the front of the room where the big TV screen stood frozen with his dad's smiling face. Fighting back his tears, and with his voice breaking, Danny began, "My dad was always my hero. Not because of any *one* thing he did, but because of how he lived his life every single day. I learned about life just by watching my dad. He was respectful to everyone. As a little boy, I remember once, my dad and I saw a homeless man on the street during a cold winter day. Dad stopped the car and got out. I thought he was going to give the man some money. Not only did Dad give him *all* the money he had in his pocket, but also he then took off his favorite leather jacket and handed it to the shivering man, shook his hand and wished him a 'Merry Christmas.' Dad just treated everyone with dignity and love. And all my life, it was so obvious that he loved my mom to the ends of the Earth and back again. And that's a great feeling for a kid," Danny said, looking at his mom, who was smiling at him, so proud of the man he'd become. "And," Danny went on, tears running down his face, "I'm gonna miss my dad, but the gifts he gave me are what I'll have for my lifetime. I just hope that one day I'll be half the father that Dad was to me!" Tears streaming steadily down his face and onto his suit jacket, Danny sat down on the ottoman that Layne had gotten up from as she'd walked to the front of the room.

Claire marveled at what a strikingly beautiful young woman her daughter had become. With shiny brown hair and deep green eyes, she looked so much like Daniel. As Layne tried to speak, her voice broke but Uncle Mark was quick to stand beside his favorite niece, with a supportive arm round her shoulder to steady her.

Clearing her throat and glancing at the image of her dad on the screen behind her, Layne said, "My dad was my world. As far back as I can remember he only wanted the best for all of us. I didn't know till years later what sacrifices he and Mom had made for us at times. Dad wanted us to see and do so much, but still, he never wanted us to take for granted all that we had. I have so many great memories of Dad," she continued, wanting to share her dad with everyone there. "Dancing around the house on Daddy's feet; learning to swim; helping Dad put up the Christmas tree lights; driving on the dirt roads in the mountains as I sat on his lap to see over the wheel and having ice cream for dinner when Mom was out of town!" (The crowd laughed at Layne's last memory, as did Claire, who heard of it for the first time in that instant.)

"But," Layne went on, "The biggest thing I'll always remember about my dad was how fiercely he loved us and our mom. He was so loving and respectful to Mom. He always treated her like a treasure."

Layne looked over at her mom who was crying, but also smiling.

"Dad wasn't here nearly long enough, but he taught us all so much," Layne said. Then, turning toward the screen behind her, she added, "I love you, Daddy," and she kissed her fingers, touching them to the image of her smiling dad, as tears ran down her cheeks.

Daniel's tribute lasted all afternoon, and into the evening, with person after person wanting to share stories of how Daniel had impacted their lives. At around six-thirty, the guests began to leave, each hugging Claire and the kids and wishing them well.

When the last guest had gone, Elaine insisted that Claire lie down. While Elaine was tossing the throw pillows from Claire's bed, Claire asked, "Hey, how did Ryan know to use our song at the end of the video?"

Elaine smiled and said, "Dan talked to him a few weeks ago. Even though he didn't know Ryan would make the video then, he wanted someone to know about the song, just in case you used music at his service."

"Daniel," Claire said, shaking her head and smiling slightly, "Always thinking of me."

Chapter 6

When Claire awoke the next morning, she realized that she'd slept all night. Tossing back the bedcovers, she saw she was still wearing her navy dress from the day before.

She showered and dressed, thankful that she'd dreamt of Daniel during the night. She actually felt refreshed and somewhat rested, which surprised her, considering the circumstances.

Her houseful of in-laws would be going home soon and the stress of the last few days would be behind her, so Claire could grieve for Daniel in her own way, which is all that she really wanted.

Everyone had flights to catch that day, all saying their good-byes, but promising to keep in touch. Claire's mother had planned to stay for another week to 'help Claire get settled' she'd said.

But Claire had insisted that Danny and Layne get back to their classes at UF, just like Daniel had wanted. And, while she was sad to see his gray Highlander turn out of their driveway, Claire knew that Danny would care for his little sister just like Daniel had always instructed him to do.

Daniel and Claire had set the kids up in a small condo near the college campus, promising to pay their expenses as long as they kept up their grades. And so far, Danny and Layne had kept up their end of the bargain, a fact that Daniel had always loved to brag on good-naturedly.

For the next few days, Claire and her mom took things slowly, giving Claire a chance to catch her breath, relieved that her house was quiet once again.

Sitting beside the pool one afternoon and sipping iced tea, Jill Douglas said, "Honey, we need to talk."

Claire braced her self. "Okay, Mom, but this sounds serious and I don't think I can **do** 'serious' at the moment."

Claire's mom swung her tanned, shapely legs over the side of her chaise lounge and sat upright, looking at Claire.

"Oh, Claire," she said, "My heart just breaks for you."

"I'll be okay, Mom," Claire told her, "We're in good shape financially. The kids' school is paid for and the house is paid off."

"No, no," Claire," her mom said, raising both hands and shaking her perfectly-coiffed head, "That's not what I mean at all. When I go home and you're all alone in this big, empty house, it'll hit you!"

Claire hadn't thought of that and now she felt panic setting in.

"Thanks, Mom," she said, rolling her eyes. "Something *else* to look forward to."

"Listen, Claire," Jill said, "I wish *I'd* had someone to talk to me about it when I lost your dad years ago. It would've been a *whole* lot easier!"

"What? You never missed a beat, Mom!" Claire said, "In fact, Eva and I noticed that you stepped up your tennis lessons and your cocktail parties, you double-booked your manicures! You didn't STOP!" Claire said, remembering how hurt she and her younger sister had been when their dad had died when they were in high school. The girls had thought their mom had been unaffected by it all.

"Oh, no, Claire!" Jill explained, "I over-scheduled my life so I wouldn't have to face the reality or the pain. I never wanted to slow down long enough to **feel**, Claire!"

"What?" Claire asked, genuinely shocked by her mom's confession.

"Listen! It was all I could do to hold it together for you and Eva!" Jill said, "I thought if I just kept busy enough, I wouldn't have *time* to let the pain in!"

"Oh, Mom! We never knew! We were just kids!" Claire said, feeling so sad for her mom now.

"It was the only way I knew how to be strong for you girls!" Jill told her. "Crazy, wasn't it? And the worst part was when my world finally came crashing down on me! You and Eva were away at college by then."

"What?" Claire asked. "What do you mean, Mom?"

"Oh, Claire," Jill went on. "I wished I'd died too! I missed your father so much! And when you girls were gone, I didn't know what to *do* with myself!"

"I see where this is going now," Claire said, nodding slowly.

"That's why I'm worried about you, Claire," her mom said, putting her hand on Claire's arm.

"What should I do then, Mom?" Claire asked, now terrified of what might lay ahead for her.

"Don't stop living, Claire! Not for a minute!" her mom told her. "And, whatever you do, don't stop **feeling**, no matter how bad things get, you work **through** it and things will get better! *Don't* ignore what you're feeling!"

Thinking about what her mom had said, Claire said, "I promise, Mom. I promise. I'm glad you finally told me this now."

Claire sat up, leaned over and hugged her mom, finally understanding what it had been like for Jill so many years ago.

"Now I know why you wanted to stay for a few days," she said, smiling at her mom.

"Well, I wasn't the best mother to you and Eva when your dad died. The least I can do is try to help *you* now!"

"You *are* the best mother!" Claire told her, hugging her again.

Chapter 7

A few days later, Claire drove her mother to the airport so Jill Douglas could return to Tennessee to her busy, over-scheduled life of golf lessons, charity work and dinner parties.

Returning home from the airport an hour later, Claire vowed to herself that she'd never allow herself to cram so much into her life that she'd stuff down her feelings – no matter how bad they might be! She'd get through this.

As she parked her Volvo in her garage, Claire realized that her house was now empty of people and that she'd have to finally face the question of what to do with Daniel's ashes.

During one of their many 'talks,' Daniel had jokingly suggested that she keep his ashes in a Crown Royal bottle on the bar in their family room, so he could still mingle at their parties.

'*Just like my Daniel*!' Claire thought to her self, recalling the memory with a slight smile.

It was after five o'clock in the evening and the setting sun illuminated the granite throughout her kitchen. Noticing how the light danced off the shimmering gold and brown stone, Claire remembered the day she and Daniel had gone to the stone yard to select the slabs to be used in their kitchen. Daniel had left the selection completely up to Claire, trusting her skills as an interior designer. And, similarly, when it came to the structural aspects of their house remodel, she deferred to Daniel. They had balanced each other perfectly, as in all things. There was a little piece of 'Daniel' in everything, Claire realized.

Looking at the clock on the wall, Claire realized she should make herself some dinner since she hadn't eaten all day. Reaching for the handle on her refrigerator, she stopped herself.

'*Why bother though*?' she thought, thinking once again about her *new* '*World of Ones*' as she regarded her new life. '*Why bother cooking for just* **one person**?'

Instead, she went to the pantry and grabbed a box of cheese crackers and then poured herself a Diet Coke. She pulled out one of the tall, swivel, high-backed bar stools at the bar in her kitchen, and for the next half hour, she read through some of the mail that had accumulated over the past week.

'*So many cards*!' she thought, opening one envelope after another, from people sending their sympathies to her and the kids.

Not yet finished opening all the envelopes, Claire caught a glimpse of the family photo albums Danny and Layne had been looking through just a week earlier. Without thinking, Claire walked over to the hutch where the albums were neatly lined up with their colorful spines visible.

She reached for one of the albums, but quickly pulled her hand back, afraid that her heart just might break if she opened the pages to the memories tucked safely and quietly inside the treasured book. Squeezing her eyes shut for a second, Claire swallowed hard, remembering her mother's advice to 'never stop feeling,' and she again reached for the album.

Quickly, and before she could change her mind, she grabbed a red, fabric-covered book and took it to the nearby kitchen table. Pulling out a chair, she kicked off her shoes, half-eager and half-afraid to re-live the memories within the book before her, so soon after losing Daniel.

Opening the album, Claire was relieved that the first page had cute photos of Danny and Layne dressed-up for Halloween many years ago. Danny was about five and Layne probably three and a half. Grinning back at Claire was a smiling little Ninja and a petite, brunette Cinderella, both holding their plastic pumpkins eager to go out trick-or-treating. Claire could see the stacks of drywall and building materials behind her kids, in the background of the photo, and she remembered that particular Halloween well.

The Mitchell house had been under construction for what had seemed like forever, so Daniel had decided to use it's horrid state to their benefit and he and Danny had turned it into their own 'haunted house.' They'd hung spider webs across the windows and skeletons from the huge oak trees in the yard and they'd staked 'Condemned' signs in the grass. Eerie music played from inside the darkened house as a strobe light flashed from inside. Danny had hated that his house had been under construction until that Halloween when he was the talk of the neighborhood with his very own 'Haunted Mansion,' as his friends had put it.

Shaking her head now and smiling to herself, Claire marveled as she remembered how Daniel could always 'make lemonade out of lemons!'

More memories jumped off the pages at Claire. There was Danny holding a trophy nearly as big as he was the year his baseball team had won the championship game. Claire remembered that Daniel had coached his team, something he'd loved doing.

Then there was little Layne standing on Daniel's shoulders in their swimming pool, holding her daddy's hands. Claire remembered that Layne had chipped her front tooth as soon as she'd jumped from Daniel's shoulders right after the photo was snapped.

And next, there was a fuzzy photo of Daniel playfully squeezing Claire and kissing her neck as she was laughing and throwing her head back. Danny had taken the photo while on a trip to the mountains, Claire remembered. She touched the photo now tenderly, remembering how all the Mitchells had loved their family trips to the mountains. Out of all the places they'd taken their children, Layne and Danny had best loved visiting the old farmhouse that Daniel's parents had left to him.

It wasn't just the beautiful scenery or the breath-taking views around their property that they'd all loved, but it was the fact that no one interrupted their 'family time' together while they were there. There was no cell phone reception there and no Internet access, which Daniel and Claire had truly loved. They had all they needed in each other. Just God's Country and the Mitchells – all they really needed to be happy.

Looking at the photo, Claire recalled that Layne had caught her first fish in the pond behind the old mountain house; and the kids used to delight in picking apples on the property and then helping Claire bake apple pies. When Danny was little, he and Daniel would go for a hike and he'd 'radio' Claire with his walkie-talkie when they were on their way back so she'd have his hot chocolate waiting.

"Good times," Claire whispered aloud, thinking she'd give anything to go back and freeze time, staying there with her family forever.

Chapter 8

A few months after Daniel had died, Claire decided to re-arrange their bedroom furniture, something she'd done from time to time during her marriage. She found her round furniture sliders and got busy one morning, shifting the bureau, the heavy dresser, her bed, the upholstered chairs in the seating area and all the decorator accents. She had hoped that the refreshed look might also somehow refresh her spirits.

Sitting down in one of the big, overstuffed chairs, she surveyed the room with all its relocated furnishings.

'*Too cramped like this,*' she decided, realizing she wanted to get rid of the big bureau in the corner. She knew that meant she'd have to empty all her sweaters and rarely worn clothes from it though, and find a new place for them. She instantly knew what else that meant: *Daniel's closet.*

She had been putting it off for months, not wanting to clean out his closet, somehow comforted just knowing that his clothes still hung there. She had, however, stopped going into the closet and sitting on the floor, surrounded by Daniel's things.

Walking to the closet, she hesitated briefly, took a deep breath and then bravely opened the door. She hadn't been in the closet for nearly a month a half, which she had considered to be progress.

Stepping into the carpeted closet, her gaze immediately went to 'the white box' on the shelf where Danny had put it for her months earlier.

"You can do this," she reassured herself aloud remembering her vow to herself to get through the awful times.

She touched the white box briefly, and then started taking Daniel's shirts, hangers and all, out to her bed. She went out to her garage to grab some empty boxes and soon she had nearly emptied Daniel's entire closet, keeping a few favorite pieces that she just couldn't force herself to part with.

Looking around the big, empty closet, Claire saw nothing but empty shelves, racks and cedar lined walls – and 'the white box,' sitting alone now on its shelf.

"Oh, Daniel," Claire said, wondering what to do with his ashes.

Then Claire heard her cell phone ringing from the bedroom. Rushing to grab it, she heard Layne's voice.

"Mom? Are you okay? You sound like you're out of breath!"

"No, I'm fine, Hon!" Claire said, trying to act cheerful. "Just cleaning closets."

"Mom, haven't you cleaned just about everything in that whole house by now?" Layne joked.

"Just about," Claire told her. "But, if I get bored, I'll come up there and start in your brother's room!"

"Yeah, and I'll help dig you out later!" Layne laughed, rolling her eyes at the thought of her brother's messy bedroom.

"Hey, Mom, listen! Danny and I are wondering what you want to do about Thanksgiving. It's not too far away," Layne said.

"Yeah, I know," Claire said reluctantly. "I'm not feeling very festive, honestly, but MeMa asked if we want to come to Tennessee, to her house this year. What do you think?"

"Yeah," Layne said. "It'd do you good, Mom. And, if you want to drive up here, we'll drive with you to Tennessee. Danny's right here, agreeing with me too!"

"Well, okay, if you two are sure," Claire said, not wanting to disappoint her children, but not wanting to acknowledge the holiday season either.

Claire talked to Layne for a while longer, and then to Danny too. Hanging up the phone, she felt better, although she still wasn't looking forward to her first holiday without Daniel.

Looking at all the boxes of Daniel's things, she decided she'd donate them to the church down the road the next day. Seeing Daniel's blue velour bathrobe on top of the box closest to her, she picked it up, unfolded it and slipped it on. The robe was huge on her, but she loved the fact that it still smelled like Daniel.

She decided she'd keep the robe and she lay down on her bed, tears filling her eyes. She quietly dozed off, with her entire body, hands and feet included, wrapped inside Daniel's cozy blue bathrobe.

A couple hours later, the sound of her ringing cell phone startled Claire. "Uh, hello?" she said groggily, after fumbling for the phone.

"Claire?" Elaine said, "You okay?"

"Fine," Claire said, "Guess I must've fallen asleep."

"Well, I thought I'd stop by tomorrow and take you to lunch!" Elaine said.

Looking down at Daniel's big, blue bathrobe, Claire said, "Oh, thanks, El, but, no, I don't think I can."

"What?" Elaine said, "Too busy? Lunch with the Queen of England again or something equally important to keep you tied-up?"

"Very funny!" Claire said, searching for a good excuse that she had not already used on her best friend, who'd been trying to get her out of the house for months. "I'm just not up to it," Claire said.

"You're up to a quick lunch with your oldest, um, I mean, 'dearest' friend!" Elaine told her. "I'll be there tomorrow at noon!"

And with that, Elaine hung up before Claire could offer another protest. Shaking her head, but smiling, Claire was thankful for Elaine's persistence.

Standing up from her bed, Claire thought 'Okay, *finish this*!' as she opened the drawers in the heavy bureau and started carrying her own sweaters to Daniel's empty closet.

Before long, the heavy bureau was empty, as she carried the last stack of lingerie to the closet. Placing a black negligee next to 'the box' Claire said, "You always did like this one, Daniel." Then, remembering that she'd worn that very negligee for Daniel one night while at their mountain house, it hit her and she knew what she'd do with Daniel's ashes.

She decided that when the weather had warmed-up and the snow had melted, she'd take Daniel's ashes back to the mountains in Virginia, to the area he'd always loved. Claire felt relieved to have made the decision.

The next day, Elaine arrived at Claire's home just before noon, as she'd promised.

"Hey, do you mind stopping by the church down the road so I can drop off Daniel's things?" Claire asked, as Elaine stepped into her living room.

"Of course not! Not at all!" Elaine said, stooping to help Claire pick-up one of the boxes neatly stacked just inside the front door.

"So, did it go okay for you?" Elaine asked, referring to cleaning out Daniel's things.

"Better than I'd hoped," Claire answered honestly. "I'd been putting it off, you know," she added, carrying a box to Elaine's waiting car at the end of the brick walk.

"What are your plans for Thanksgiving?" Elaine asked.

"Going to Mom's with the kids," Claire said.

"Good! That's great actually!" Elaine said, glad to hear Claire was finally going to be leaving her house.

After dropping off Daniel's clothes at the church, the two women went to a quiet, little restaurant situated along the river and just a few miles south of Claire's house.

Over huge salads and glasses of Chardonnay, the two old friends easily chatted for a couple hours.

"So, what are your plans?" Elaine asked.

"Good Lord!" Claire said, irritably. "Must I have a *plan*?"

"Uh, well, no, Sorry," Elaine said, shocked at Claire's outburst.

"No, **I'm** sorry, El," Claire said, putting her fork down. "It's just that I don't know what to do with myself next! When Daniel was here, we always had plans, and now I don't even want to think past *tomorrow*!"

"Well, you know, maybe *that's* okay too," Elaine tried to reassure her friend. "Who says there's a playbook for you to follow, anyway?"

"Really, El, if it weren't for the kids, I don't think I could even face another tomorrow without Daniel," Claire said, hopelessly. "There's truly no point."

"Don't say that, Claire!" Elaine told her. "You're important to too many people! Don't you even **think** like that!"

"God, I'm really sorry," Claire said, shaking her head. "I don't mean to burden you with all this."

"You could *never* burden me, Hon," Elaine said, putting her hand on Claire's arm that rested on the table as she fumbled with her salad again.

"Listen, Claire, if Daniel were here right now, what would be going on in your lives at this time of year?" Elaine asked.

"Besides the obvious upcoming holiday plans, I mean."

Thinking for a minute, Claire smiled slightly and said, "Well, we'd have just gotten back from the mountain house about a month ago and of course we'd be planning for Thanksgiving and a big family Christmas, which I will not even **begin** to let myself think about."

"Okay," Elaine began slowly. "Well, for starters, you and the kids will be having Christmas with Ryan and me."

"Oh, no, El," Claire said. "The kids have had this big ski trip planned with their friends from college since before Daniel even got so sick. I've absolutely insisted that they stick to their plans."

"You've *got* to be kidding me!" Elaine said, shocked that Claire would be without Danny and Layne during her first Christmas with Daniel, too.

"The kids fought me on it, too, but I won't let them change their plans," Claire said. "It'll actually make Christmas easier for them if they're not in the house without their dad in it right now."

"Yeah, well, *maybe*," Elaine said. "But what about **you**? You're coming to *my house* then!"

"No, actually, I think I just decided in the last five minutes what I'm going to do at Christmastime! And *you've* helped me to decide!" Claire said.

"Oh, great!" Elaine said, "Here were go with that impetuous side of you again! What's your plan?"

"Well, I decided last night that I should take Daniel's ashes back up to the mountains in Virginia eventually, and you just asked what we'd be doing this time of year if Daniel were still here," Claire explained, "So, maybe it'd be good for me to go up to the mountain house for a few weeks."

"But, you can't spread his ashes till the spring, right? I mean the ground is probably frozen now!" Elaine said.

"Yeah," Claire said, but I can take the ashes up there. And, besides, it'll do me good to spend a little time learning how to be by myself, getting to know myself. I mean, El, I've never lived alone – ever!"

"Claire, you're a born and bred Florida Girl! You're **not** going to go poking around icy, mountainous roads all by yourself!" Elaine protested. "Daniel would never have wanted you to do that!"

"I'll be fine," Claire told her closest friend, for whom she'd named her own daughter. "I'll drive the SUV. It's four-wheel drive."

"Oh, I feel much better," Elaine said dryly, taking a sip of her wine, then shaking her head at her stubborn friend's insistence.

An hour later, Elaine dropped Claire back at her home, hugging her good-bye. "Claire," she said sincerely, "Please promise you'll call if you need anything – even if you need to talk at 2:00 in the morning!"

"I promise! And thanks for lunch! I feel like my head is somewhat cleared now! I needed that!" Claire said, stepping from Elaine's car and then waving gratefully as Elaine backed down her driveway.

Chapter 9

One afternoon, just as Claire was beginning to panic when she couldn't find yet another project with which to busy her self, she remembered that she could still organize her attic. Relieved to have a task to occupy her mind, she headed directly upstairs and into the second floor hall, then up another steeper set of steps to the big attic.

Opening the heavy wooden door and switching on the light, Claire was at once hit with the familiar sights and scents of the past. Ski clothes hung neatly on garment racks with ski boots lined-up underneath and colorful ski helmets on a shelf across the top of the racks. A huge, floor-to-ceiling bookcase was jammed with dozens of stuffed animals that Layne had refused to part with, even when she'd left for college. The dollhouse that Daniel had built for Layne sat on a table waiting to one day get passed down to Layne's own daughter. Danny's old football helmet and cleats were on a nearby shelf and his lacrosse sticks were propped nearby.

Claire stood still, her eyes continuing to canvass the cavernous room.

Her sewing machine sat on a crafts table, unused for years, next to her easel that she hadn't painted at since Layne was about ten.

She stood in one spot, slowly turning in a full circle and taking in memory after memory around her, till her gaze fell on a wooden chest at the end of the long room that ran the length of the entire house.

Instantly recognizing the wood piece, she slowly walked over to it and knelt beside it, running her hand across the top of the beautiful hand-stained piece. Lifting its heavy lid, Claire reached in and pulled out the first item on top, a neatly folded quilt. She pulled it to her face, closed her eyes and inhaled its scent deeply, remembering the day she'd bought the treasured quilt.

*

She and Daniel had been on a car trip with little Danny buckled in his car seat in the back behind them. Danny had been cranky and was tired of riding in the car on their long drive to Floyd, Virginia.

Daniel had suggested, "Let's pull-off and let him run around for a while."

Agreeing, Claire pointed to a small cottage-style shop along the country roadside.

"How 'bout here?" she said.

Laughing at her 'retail radar' as he called it, Daniel replied jokingly, "I once heard that Ben Franklin said 'Beware any endeavor that requires a new set of clothes' and *this* looks like a boutique!"

"Well," Claire said laughing and stepping from the car, "Aren't we lucky Ben's not here then?"

"You go ahead," Daniel had told her, smiling, "I'll let Danny stretch his legs."

"Just let me know when you boys are ready to go!" she said heading for the door of the quaint little shop.

Pushing the white wooden door open, Claire jumped at the sudden sound of the jingling chimes overhead. An older woman's voice called out from the back, "Hello! And welcome!"

"Oh, thank you!" Claire said, barely seeing the top of the white-haired woman's head above a shelf toward the back of the store.

Walking in, she could see the little shop was filled with hand-made treasures. Crochet doilies; knitted afghan throws; pretty aprons that were much too beautiful to cook in; all types of pottery obviously from various artisans; watercolors and needlepoint crafts were in every available nook and cranny. The offerings never ended as Claire looked around appreciating all the beautiful things.

Looking up on a wall, Claire saw a gorgeous hand-made quilt hanging near the elderly, sweet-faced shopkeeper.

"Oh! That is incredible!" she exclaimed.

"Well, thank you, my dear!" the smiling woman said proudly. "That's one of mine actually! The pattern is called 'The Love Knot.' See how the rings all intertwine?"

"It's just beautiful!" Claire told her, admiring the delicate handwork.

The front door opened suddenly, jingling the chimes once again. Looking toward the sound, Claire said, "Daniel, come and see this!"

Walking back toward her, he glanced toward the quilt distractedly, holding Daniel on his shoulders. "Mmmm," he said, then glanced at his watch, intent on getting to the mountain house in time for the kick-off of the big game that afternoon.

"Daniel, I just have to take it home with us!" Claire said, trying to ignite his interest.

"Sure. Okay," he said, unaware of the price tag for such an exquisite, handmade piece. "I'll just put Danny in the car and meet you outside."

Minutes later, Claire was back in the car beside Daniel and they were pulling back onto the road. She had her prized quilt on her lap and was holding it up admiring the intricate work in the paisley, floral and plaid piece, with it's rose, blue and green shades.

"Oh! I just can't wait to put this on the bed in the mountain house! It's perfect!" she said, "Can you believe it was only $750?"

"What?!" Daniel said nearly driving off the side of the road as he winced. "Are you kidding me?!"

"Daniel, this is a collector's dream! One-of-a-kind!" Claire tried to explain. "We'll have this quilt in our family for years!"

"Well, good thing we'll have it this winter, since we won't be able to pay our electric bill!" he said half-jokingly, but still in shock.

Claire smiled, knowing the quilt had been an extravagance, but she was also thrilled with her priceless find.

After arriving at the mountain house that Daniel's parents had left to him when they'd died years earlier, Claire carried a sleepy Danny upstairs for a nap while Daniel carried their luggage inside.

Calling downstairs, Claire asked, "Hon, can you turn on the heat? It's chilly up here!"

"Got it!" he answered.

A few minutes later, Claire smiled as she heard the sound of the football game coming from the living room below. After Danny had fallen asleep, Claire covered him, put the baby gate at the top of the stairs and tiptoed downstairs, eager to put her new, treasured quilt on the bed in the master bedroom.

Minutes later, standing back from the bed and admiring the quilt, Claire felt Daniel come up behind her, wrapping his arms around her waist and nuzzling her neck.

"Isn't is just beautiful?" Claire said looking at the quilt.

"You certainly are, Love," Daniel said, turning her around to face him so he could kiss her.

Filled with warmth although the house was still cool, Claire reached up, encircling Daniel's neck with both arms and kissing him passionately. Gently guiding her backward toward the bed, Daniel lifted Claire and slowly laid her on the bed, still kissing her.

"Um, what about your game?" Claire said.

"Don't you worry! I've brought my game!" Daniel answered playfully, kissing her again and unbuttoning her blouse.

An hour later, as they lay beneath the beautiful new quilt, their clothes piled on the floor beside the bed, Daniel said, "Oh, by the way, I think I really love your new quilt!"

They both started laughing as Daniel cuddled her closer and they lay staring out the window at the full moon that had

risen just over the treetops beyond the
window.

*

Not even realizing she had wrapped
the quilt around her shoulders while she'd
reminisced, Claire leaned against the wall
beside the open chest. The afternoon sun's
rays shone through a dormer window onto
the brown etched carving in the corner of
the chest's open lid. "**FOREVER** " it read,
bringing tears to Claire's eyes.

She remembered their first Christmas
together when Daniel had built her the
chest. It had been the only gift he could
afford to give her on his meager salary
back then, but it was truly one of the
best things he'd ever given to her.

Wishing she could go back to that
simple Christmas when they'd made love
throughout the day, watched old holiday
movies and eaten roast chicken in their
tiny apartment, Claire said aloud, "Yes,
it *was* a 'Wonderful Life,' Daniel. Just
way too short." The tears silently slid
down her cheeks as she ached for her
Daniel.

Startled suddenly, Claire jumped
slightly at the sound of the door chimes
downstairs. She stepped toward a nearby
dormer window to have a look outside and
saw a large blue sedan parked on her brick
driveway below.

Because she was directly above the front porch, Claire couldn't see who was ringing her doorbell. '*Salesman,*' she thought to herself, deciding to ignore the intrusion. But a minute later, the insistent chimes started again.

"Alright, already!" she said aloud, heading toward the stairs, just as the melodic chimes stopped ringing. Rounding the second landing I her bare feet, Claire could see a professionally-dressed older man standing on her front porch through the front sidelight window beside the door.

Still sure he was a salesman, Claire cracked the door slightly and asked, "Yes?" suddenly aware that her mascara must be streaked down her face.

"Good afternoon, Ma'am," replied the kind-faced older man, taking a step backward, so as to make Claire more comfortable, "Would you happen to be Dan's wife – er – widow, Claire Mitchell?"

"I am," Claire told him, wincing a bit at the label of 'widow.'

"Well," the man went on, taking a card from his inside jacket pocket and showing it to Claire, "I'm Sam Eaton with Winston & Eaton here in town."

"Oh, yes," Claire nodded, remembering hearing Daniel speak of the man.

"Well," Mr. Eaton went on, "Your husband had asked that our firm assist you in administering his trust and that we make sure that you and the children are comfortable in every way."

"I see," Claire said, amazed that Daniel's planning was still coming to the surface even months after his death.

"Won't you please come in?" she offered, opening the door fully. "We can sit over here," she said, gesturing to the seating area beside the fireplace in the living room.

Taking her seat, she was suddenly very uncomfortable in her bare feet and mascara-streaked face as she sat with the nice man in his neatly pressed suit.

"I know you've already received several bulk pay-outs from the life insurance policies and I've put the proceeds from the company's buy-sell agreement into the trust, as Dan had instructed," he said, handing her a manila folder. "And of course there are annuities, some stocks, and the income from the commercial rental properties." "Dan has left you and the children in *great* shape!" Mr. Eaton went on.

"He always took such good care of us," Claire said.

"Well, just so you know, the money in the trust belongs solely to you, Claire and then to the children, of course, upon your death. Our firm is merely the administrator. You'll receive sizable quarterly pay-outs from the trust."

"Well, thank you," Claire said, "I really don't even know what plans I have at this time. The house is paid off the house and so is kids' schooling. But, right now, I just can't make any more decisions."

"I understand and that's fine. I just wanted to make an introduction. Whenever you need us, you know how to reach us!" Mr. Eaton said, and rose to leave, as he handed Claire his business card.

Claire thanked him for coming out, shaking his hand as she walked him to the front door.

Standing on her covered front porch, Claire waved goodbye to Mr. Eaton as he backed his sedan down the long brick driveway. Stepping toward the front door, she glanced at the two white rockers on her front porch. Hesitantly, she walked over to one and ran her hand along the edge of one of the arms on the rocker, remembering the hours she and Daniel had rocked away on that porch over the years.

Feeling her chest tighten, Claire sat down in the rocker, immediately drawing her knees to her chest and putting her feet on the seat with her chin on her knees. She looked out at the peaceful, still river.

Rocking slowly, she remembered the countless cool, crisp winter nights she and Daniel had sat side-by-side watching the moonlight's reflection on the river.

And the early mornings they'd sat quietly drinking their coffee and reading the newspaper together on the porch before the kids woke up. And the lazy summer afternoons they'd sat watching Danny and Layne play in the yard with their friends.

'So many good times,' Claire thought, *'Now only distant memories.'*

Chapter 10

Thanksgiving proved to be mercifully better than Claire had expected. Driving to her mom's home in Tennessee was just what she and Danny and Layne had needed.

Taking turns driving back, after the holiday, they talked the entire trip, exchanging stories about Daniel, alternately laughing and crying.

After dropping Danny and Layne back at their condo in Gainesville, Claire turned her car toward the highway, determined to drive straight through and return home later that day. She'd vowed to herself to be strong when she got home to the big, empty house hours later and she didn't want to put it off for a minute.

Later that evening, as she turned her car into her driveway, Claire caught sight of her swimming pool. The water's surface was covered with yellow-green algae. *'Great,'* Claire thought to her self, *'Guess I'll finally be learning how that pool pump works.'*

With Daniel gone, Claire had been determined to learn to do things for herself, and in recent months she'd cleaned the gutters; changed a tire herself; mounted a ceiling fan and even fixed her own garbage disposal, all to the dismay of her children who couldn't understand why she refused to call repairmen for these things.

Pulling her wheeled suitcase behind her through the garage, Claire reached for the door handle to the laundry room to enter her house, and then abruptly stopped. She shuddered to realize that this was the first time in her life that she'd come home from a holiday without Daniel.

'*Another first,*' she thought, swallowing hard.

Mustering her courage, she pushed the lever handle on the door and walked into her house. As she pulled her suitcase into the kitchen, Claire glanced at her blinking answering machine. Dropping her keys beside it, she pushed the red, blinking button.

"Hey, Hon!" the cheerful voice said, "It's Elaine! Just checking to see how your trip went! Call me!"

There were a half dozen other messages from friends and family and one from Mr. Wimbley in Floyd, Virginia.

"Claire? You, there, Claire?" the friendly, old voice said, pausing to see if Claire might pick up the phone, "Uh, Claire, it's James Wimbley up here. Got your message that you'll be comin' up soon! I'll open up your place and check things out before you get here. Now you be careful on the drive up! These roads can be tricky!"

Claire smiled as she thought of old Mr. Wimbley who'd been a friend of her family's for over twenty years and had even known Daniel's parents when they were alive. He and his wife lived down the dirt road from the Mitchell's mountain house and kept an eye on their place for them.

Exhausted from her drive, Claire decided to phone Elaine back in the morning, opting instead for a hot shower and a good night's sleep, without even bothering to eat dinner.

When she awoke the next morning, Elaine phoned before Claire could even make her first cup of coffee.

"So you *did* make it home, I see!" Elaine said.

"Hey, El," Claire said, "Sorry I didn't call last night. I was exhausted when I got in. I drove straight through."

"No worries! I figured as much!" Elaine said. "You can make it up to me by coming shopping with me today."

"Oh, no!" Claire said, "I'm not up for one your marathon shopping sprees! No way!"

"Okay, then. How about just lunch?" Elaine said hopefully.

"Okay, but not too early!" Claire said, not wanting to disappoint her best friend, but not really wanting to meet for lunch either.

"Well, how about we meet about 2:00 at Opus?" Elaine asked. "And I'll go shopping first. I really need to find something for Ryan for Christmas …… Oh, sorry, Claire, I, uh, I didn't think…"

"No, no," Claire said, wishing that **she** still had a husband to shop for. "It's fine, really."

Sighing, Elaine said, "Then 2:00 it is. I'll see you there!"

Hanging up the phone, Claire realized that under ordinary circumstances her home would already be fully decorated for the holidays. Daniel would have strung lights outside. She'd have decorated every inch of the house's interior, not missing an opportunity to hang a bit of Christmas cheer in any corner.

Most years would have seen a Mitchell Christmas party in the huge house with wall-to-wall friends and family. And she would have welcomed a call from Elaine to go Christmas shopping and grab a lunch with her best girlfriend. But now, it all seemed barely a distant memory, as if she had only a glimpse of someone else's charmed, happy life.

Claire had resolved in early November that she would not put up any holiday decorations or even acknowledge the Christmas holiday that year, thinking it would make it easier for her to get through the season without Daniel if she denied all the holiday trimmings. Part of the reason she'd insisted that Danny and Layne stick to their holiday ski trip plans was really so they wouldn't have to see how depressed their mom was feeling.

But, she'd promised Elaine to meet for lunch, and instantly she'd regretted giving in to Elaine's persuasiveness, preferring instead to curl-up on her sofa.

Hours later though, Claire walked into Opus and saw Elaine waving from a booth in the back of the quaint restaurant.

"Hey there!" Elaine said, smiling and getting up to hug Claire.

"Looks like you've got quite a haul there already!" Claire said, referring to the half-dozen shopping bags in the booth beside Elaine.

"Yeah, I've done some damage!" Elaine said.

Sliding into the booth again, Elaine pushed a tall glass toward Claire on the tabletop.

"I ordered you a pomegranate iced tea."

"Perfect," Claire said, sipping the tea.

"And they have the almond-encrusted salmon with whipped chive potatoes that you always like," Elaine said, hoping to entice her thin friend to eat.

"Oh, I'm really not hungry," Claire said.

"Claire, you're *not* eating, are you?" Elaine asked, sighing and noticing that Claire had obviously lost even more weight.

"Here and there, you know," Claire said. "I really don't have an appetite, that's all. I'm fine."

"You've *got* to eat though," Elaine said. "Order the salmon and at least pick at it. You can take the leftovers home for later."

"I thought I just left my *mother* back in Tennessee!" Claire said sarcastically, shaking her head, but smiling at her friend, as she closed her menu.

"So tell me how things are going," Elaine asked buttering a warm yeast roll, then putting it on Claire's bread plate.

"It's so much harder than anyone could ever imagine," Claire said, sighing. "I can't even begin to explain it. I feel like I don't even know who I am now! I mean for my whole adult life I was with Daniel. I knew where I fit in to the world! I belonged with Daniel. I'm so lost now, El!"

Seeing the sadness in Claire's eyes, Elaine said, "It'll get better, Claire. It's only been a few months now. You're still getting used to all this."

"I know," Claire said, "And I hate it. I absolutely hate being here without Daniel."

Both women's eyes filled with tears as Elaine reached across the table and put her hand on top of Claire's.

"You still have lots of people who *are* here for you Claire," she said. "Don't you forget that!"

"I know. I know," Claire said, more grateful than ever for her friend. "I really don't know what I'd do without you and the kids," she added.

Elaine and Claire ordered lunch and Claire ate only a few bites of hers, so Elaine insisted she take the rest home for dinner.

"Listen, let's walk around and window shop for a while," she said after paying the check.

"Well… " Claire hesitated, "Maybe just for a little bit." She really wanted no part of the happy scenes outside of the restaurant.

But, only minutes later, as they walked along the sidewalk, Claire was overwhelmed with all the holiday sights. It was like sensory overload coming at her from all directions. Festive wreaths hung on the doors of the quaint shops. Red bows were tied atop the old-fashioned black lampposts lining the sidewalks. Twinkling lights cheerfully sparkled in the trees overhead. Holiday music was piped from stores out onto the sidewalks. Shoppers bustled about carrying bags and gift-wrapped boxes. Couples walked arm-in-arm, one stopping for a quick kiss.

It was all just too much for Claire. "Elaine," she said, stopping to sit on a nearby bench, breathing shallowly, "I just - I just *can't*!"

"Claire, I'm so sorry," Elaine said, sitting next to her and putting an arm around Claire's shoulder as she cried.

"I just miss him so *much*," Claire cried, "It actually hurts to even *breathe*, El!"

"Come on, Hon," Elaine said, "I'm taking you home. I don't know what I was thinking. I'm sorry. Ryan and I will come back for your car later. I'll drive you home."

Elaine took Claire home, helped her change into her comfy gray sweats and made her a cup of chamomile tea. Then she tucked her into bed and sat with her, while Claire dozed off and on for hours.

When Claire awoke around 2:00am, Elaine was asleep in one of the overstuffed chairs near Claire's bed. Looking at her sleeping friend, Claire realized that she *did* have people who truly still needed her and cared for her.

Elaine stirred, opening her eyes, "Hey," she said, stretching, "How're you doing?"

"Better," Claire said, "Sorry for the meltdown." "Are you kidding?" Elaine told her, **"I'm** sorry. I should've never put you in that situation. I wasn't thinking."

"None of us has been here before, dealing with this stuff," Claire said. "Hey, you really need to go home, El. It's late."

"No way," Elaine protested, "I'm not leaving you now."

"Okay," Claire said, "Will you at *least* sleep in one of the guest bedrooms upstairs? That chair can't be comfortable!"

"Now, **that** I will do!" Elaine said, laughing a bit and rubbing her neck. "But, only if you're sure you're okay."

"I'm good, really," Claire told her as Elaine stood and reached over hug her, "And thanks, El. You're such a good friend to me."

"That's what friends are for," Elaine said, thankful to see Claire feeling better.

Chapter 11

A couple weeks later, Claire loaded her suitcase in to Daniel's SUV. Walking back inside the house one last time she knew there was just one more thing she needed to pack.

Her legs felt like lead as she slowly walked to her bedroom and went to Daniel's closet. She hesitantly reached for the white box then hugged it close to her chest.

"Oh, Daniel," she whispered, closing her eyes.

Carrying the box to the garage, she went to the back of the open SUV to place it inside, beside her luggage. '*No!*' she thought, '*You are **not** cargo, my love!*'

She walked to the front passenger door and opened it, placing the box carefully on the front seat. Looking at the little box, Claire's heart physically ached, as she realized this would be their last trip to the mountain house together.

Claire drove straight through, and 11 hours later, was turning onto the Blue Ridge Parkway at dusk. There was snow, but as predicted, the main road had been cleared.

Shifting the car into four-wheel drive, Claire continued on the familiar drive, up the winding mountain road. Few cars were on the road and most businesses had closed for the winter.

Claire and Daniel usually visited the mountains in the spring or fall months. Claire wondered how anyone could live through the winters in such cold, barren conditions. A spectacular sight in the fall, the landscape now looked so still and lifeless, much like how Claire felt inside, she realized. Still, cold, lifeless and lonely.

Continuing on the winding road through the mountains, Claire passed the old mill, the winery, and the park ranger station. Each landmark held a memory of times so long ago, when Claire and Daniel had visited the area with their kids. Each sign on the tiny quaint mountain shops read: *"Closed, Closed, Closed "* just like Claire's heart felt. She literally felt like she blended into the scenery outside of her car.

Thirty minutes later, Claire turned the SUV onto the dirt and gravel road that led to the simple country-style house that Daniel's parents had left to him years before. Darkness blanketed the landscape as a light fog rolled in, causing Claire to drive even slower than usual.

She'd switched off the radio miles earlier when she'd lost the signal, and the car was eerily quiet, save for the tires rolling slowly along the icy, dirt and gravel road. Suddenly conscious of just how alone she felt, Claire shifted in her seat uneasily and turned up the car's heater, as she carefully made her way along the dark narrow road.

Minutes later, relief washed over her as she saw the lights on at her house in the distance. "Mr. Wimbley," Claire murmured, smiling slightly as she realized her old friend had left the lights on for her at her house.

Putting her car in *park*, Claire's eyes immediately fell to the house's back porch, her gaze settling on two old, weathered wooden rockers. Just as they had at that their home in Florida, she and Daniel had spent countless nights rocking quietly and watching the moon from the back porch.

Sometimes they'd talk, but sometimes they'd just hold hands, rocking silently, side by side. Layne had seen her first shooting star from that porch. Danny had learned to read on that very porch so many years before. Claire wished desperately that she could go back to those simple, precious times with Daniel and their children, never to leave the mountain house again.

Opening her car door, Claire stepped down onto the icy ground and heard a crunch underfoot. She carefully made her way up the wooden back steps and slid her key into the heavy old lock. Turning the heavy metal knob, she remembered the old door would stick at times, so she nudged it with her shoulder.

As the door opened, Claire was immediately hit with the familiar scents of the past. There were the original wood plank floors; the paneled walls; the solid wood cabinetry with too many coats of stain and varnish to count and the cozy wool rug that Daniel's mother had so loved. Claire remembered once reading that one's sense of smell evoked the strongest of memories and she knew it to be true at that very moment.

Mr. Wimbley had left a lamp on for her in the living room and had obviously turned on the heat because the house felt comfortable. Claire walked through the downstairs, looking around, the key still in her hand.

She stopped and sat down on the dated, green sofa and thought, *'Okay, I've made it here. **Now** what?'* as she looked around at the familiar sights.

Daniel's father's classic book collection was still proudly displayed in the hand-carved cabinet he'd crafted when Daniel was just a baby. The doilies that Daniel's mother had crocheted were still neatly laid out on the end tables as they had been for years. Even Daniel's fishing rod was leaned neatly in the corner, right where he'd left it so long ago, after showing off his catch and posing for photos at Claire's insistence.

'All the memories,' Claire thought.

Even the deep gouge in the wood floor near the stairs held a special memory for Claire. Little Danny, then only four, had dropped Daniel's mother's heavy old waffle iron on it as he'd carried it to Claire, urging her to wake up at nearly 4 AM and cook him some waffles. She and Daniel had laughed and put Danny in bed between them, both snuggling him and coaxing him back to sleep for a while. 'Sweet times,' she thought.

"Okay, so **why** did I come up here?" Claire spoke aloud, realizing that the old house held nothing but memories in every corner.

Hungry, for once, but too tired to even make her self a snack with her leftover travel foods, Claire decided to simply turn-in for the night.

'One more thing,' she thought, realizing that she still needed to carry Daniel's ashes inside and out of the cold. She took a deep breath and went outside.

Stoically, but with her heart pounding, Claire carried the white box inside, and into the bedroom. She placed it atop the tall chest in the bedroom.

Exhausted both physically and emotionally, Claire slept deeply for the first time in months.

She awoke early, with the morning sunlight streaming through the lacy sheers hanging on the bedroom windows. She stretched and pulled the big white down comforter tighter around her, wanting to soak-in the safe, still morning.

Claire closed her eyes, wishing she smelled bacon cooking in the kitchen and that Daniel would walk in at any moment with a mug of hot coffee, telling her of their plans for the day.

Opening her eyes, Claire caught sight of the white box on the tall chest in the corner of the room and was immediately shaken back into her new reality. Exhaling deeply, she threw back the covers and got up stepping into her cozy slippers she'd left beside her bed.

Walking to the window, Claire pulled back the lacy sheers, revealing the wondrous scenery outside. More snow had fallen overnight, blanketing the trees and the ground. Leaning into the window for a better look, she felt a cool draft coming in where the seal had apparently broken at the window's frame.

'Mental note to have the window fixed,' she thought, and walked from the bedroom to the kitchen to make a cup of instant coffee, hoping to find the familiar red jar still in the cabinet. She didn't care whether the coffee was fresh or not, so long as it smelled like coffee.

Suddenly the phone rang and startled Claire, causing her to jump with its shrill sound that reverberated throughout the old house. The phone in the mountain house was the same old green one Daniel's mother had installed so many years before, on the kitchen wall.

"Hello?" Claire said, curious as to who might even *know* she was at the house.

"Claire!" said the kindly, old voice. "You made it!"

"Mr. Wimbley! Good morning!" Claire said, smiling slightly. "And thank you for opening up the house and leaving some lights on for me," remembering his kindness.

"Happy to do it, Claire," he answered. "You know, you're like family to us, Hon."

"You and Mrs. Wimbley are one of the reasons we've always loved to come up here!" Claire told him.

"Well, Hon, we just wanted to make sure you got in okay! If you need anything, you just give us a jingle!" Mr. Wimbley offered.

"Well, I was actually just thinking of fixing the drafty windows in this old place," Claire mentioned. "Do you know of a reliable outfit who I could call?"

"Got just the man for the job!" he quickly told her. "Name is Matt. And he's been 'round here for a bit now," Mr. Wimbley went on. "Now he took pretty ill, a while back and had to go into the city to see the doctors there. Stayed with his sister while he recuperated. But he's good as new now! And a real nice boy too!" he continued, chuckling, as Claire imagined Mr. Wimbley's sparkling bright, blue eyes. "Tell you what, Claire, I'll ring him up for you, and send him over to your place."

"Okay, thanks! That would be great!" Claire told the helpful old man. After thanking Mr. Wimbley once again, Claire hung up the phone on the wall.

She heated a mug of water in the microwave, and made her morning coffee. Mug in hand, she pushed open the heavy door at the back of the kitchen, and heard the familiar squeak the old door had made for years.

Pulling the fleece collar of her robe up around her neck, Claire sat down one of the old, wooden rockers on the back porch. The steam rose from her mug and Claire could see her breath in the cold morning air.

Rocking slowly and gazing across the partially frozen pond, she sighed, physically aching to feel Daniel in the rocker right beside her. She longed to reach out and take his hand, silently welcoming the promise of a new day.

There'd been so many mornings, when she and Daniel had sat together in that very spot, sharing their first cup of morning coffee, making plans to go hiking, trout fishing or picnicking. Now, with the whole day in front of her, Claire had absolutely no idea what to even *do* with herself. And, she wondered if it had been such a good idea for her even to come to the mountain house alone.

"Well," she spoke aloud, "You're here now, so make the most of it."

And with that, Claire went inside to shower and dress for the day ahead, whatever it might hold in store for her.

In earlier times, Daniel would have already outlined their plans for the day, been fully dressed, himself and would playfully be prodding Claire to get a move on so they could start their day's activities. Then, there were also those lazy mornings, when Daniel and Claire would wake early, trying not to awaken their sleeping children upstairs. They'd make love in their cozy bedroom, uninterrupted in the wee morning hours as the sun came up over the treetops.

Claire had always loved their quiet times together, tucked away in the comfy old house that seemed untouched by time. Both she and Daniel had always loved the fact that their cell phones did not get reception at the house, so Daniel's employees couldn't intrude on their special times. Her own decorating clients were unable to reach her. And there was no Internet service available at the house.

For some people these things would have been considered to be major inconveniences. However, for Claire and Daniel, these were some of the very reasons they had always loved to visit the mountain house.

Chapter 12

Later that morning, Claire was stepping from the cast iron tub in the little bathroom, located just off the kitchen. As she reached for the big yellow towel she'd laid atop the wicker hamper, her gaze caught sight of a green toothbrush hanging in the holder beside the sink.

"*Daniel's*," she murmured in a hushed voice as she slowly reached for the toothbrush, entirely forgetting about her towel. Standing there, dripping water onto the floor, Claire burst into tears as she held the toothbrush to her chest. Big, heavy sobs wracked her body, as she realized that Daniel had used the toothbrush on their last trip to the house, when all was well, and they hadn't even known yet that he was sick.

Tears streamed down her face, down her neck and onto her bare chest. Feeling unsteady, she grabbed a corner of the white pedestal sink and sat down, naked, on the cold closed toilet seat behind her, still holding the toothbrush in one hand.

Composing her self, Claire decided to use Daniel's toothbrush, hoping in some insane way, to feel him with her again.

After brushing her teeth, she rinsed the toothbrush then laughed at herself through her now slower streaming tears, as she realized how crazy an idea it had been in the first place. She replaced the toothbrush in its holder again, wondering if she'd want to use it later.

Finally, Claire toweled off, then wrapped the big, oversized butter yellow towel around her self and secured it tightly, tucking in the towel's corner at her chest. Noting her red eyes in the mirror, she splashed icy cold water on her face at the sink and dried her face with a hand towel that was hanging nearby.

Opening the bathroom door, Claire was immediately startled. "Ahhh!" she screamed at the sight of a strange man in her kitchen, just a few feet away.

"Who…. Who **are** you?!" she shrieked, holding her towel more tightly, and stepping back. "What do you **want**?!"

"I… I'm… I'm sorry, ma'am," he said, putting his hands up with palms facing Claire. "I - I, uh, I didn't mean to frighten you. I thought you'd gone out for a walk or something," he stammered.

"So you were just going to rob my house while I was out?" Claire demanded.

"No, no!" he explained, "James – er- I mean 'Mr. Wimbley' asked me to come over and see about your windows."

"Oh, yes," Claire recollected, relieved that also that the stranger knew Mr. Wimbley. "Well, you scared me to death!" she added. "How'd you get in here anyway?" she demanded.

"Mr. Wimbley told me where the spare key was under the big pot on the back porch," he told her.

"You nearly scared me to death! My heart about jumped out of my chest!" Claire said, suddenly feeling awkward and naked in just her towel. She instantly felt embarrassed by her wet, dripping hair and puffy, red eyes.

"Believe me," the man said, "All this is a bit much for my **own** heart to take, too! Uh, why don't I come back later?" And with that, he put on his blue, knit cap and turned to leave.

"Yes, that might be better," Claire agreed, nodding gratefully. She then stepped toward the door to lock it as the man left. Looking through the door's small glass window, she watched as a newer model, red truck pulled away from her house. She could hear the tires crackle on the icy ground, reminding her that she was freezing herself.

Realizing she was actually shivering, Claire retrieved her slippers from the bathroom and slipped them on and then went to her bedroom to dress.

She chose denim jeans and a heavy taupe knit turtleneck sweater from her suitcase. Slipping the sweater over her head, Claire caught sight of herself in the full-length mirror that Daniel's grandfather had made decades earlier.

Surveying her own reflection, she realized that she'd finally lost those last, nagging few pounds she'd battled with for years. Although she'd always been critical of her own figure, Daniel had always loved her feminine curves, and couldn't resist running his hands over her shapely hips or kissing the nape of her neck.

How she *wished* she could feel Daniel walk up behind her now, wrapping her in his arms just one more time. She wondered, in that moment, if people really died from a broken heart, because she was certain that it was a real possibility for her.

After unpacking her suitcase, Claire when out to the SUV and brought in the various odds and ends she had packed for her trip. She'd brought along new sheet sets for all the bedrooms, a DVD player and about a dozen movies that she'd intended to watch. She'd even brought along the huge pile of unopened mail from her kitchen counter at home, assuming that most of it sympathy cards. And there were the small, wrapped Christmas gifts that Danny and Layne had insisted she take along with her.

She'd also brought back her beautiful, beloved quilt that she'd come across in her attic at home in Florida. She'd taken the quilt home to Florida several years earlier, after bundling up in it while Daniel drove the family home.

Carrying the neatly folded quilt, Claire was in awe, as always, at the delicate and skillful work throughout the piece. She'd always wondered what became of the kindly old woman who'd lovingly stitched the quilt, carefully and precisely placing each tiny stitch in the beautiful creation, and then trimming its edges with an ecru-colored eyelet fabric, a dainty touch that Claire had always appreciated.

Walking into the living room, Claire placed the quilt on the sofa beside the box of movies she'd placed there, assuming she'd curl up later and watch one, in hopes of distracting her mind.

Chapter 13

The days passed slowly, each blending into the next, but Claire felt like she was getting stronger. She realized that maybe the trip had been a good idea after all.

On Christmas Eve, Danny called to tell her that he and Layne and their friends had made it safely to Aspen and were "tearing up the slopes," as he'd put it. After a few minutes, Layne got on the phone and reminded her mom to open her gifts in the morning.

"I will, Honey," Claire promised, "And how did you and Danny like the new ski jackets I got you guys?"

"Oh, my gosh, Mom!" Layne said excitedly. "They were just perfect! Thanks!"

"Well, you two be careful out there!" Claire told her daughter. "And I love you both!"

"We love you too, Mom!" Layne said, trying not to bring up her dad so as not to upset her mother on Christmas Eve.

Hanging up the phone, Claire suddenly wished the kids were with her. She decided to put in a DVD and watch a movie to occupy her thoughts.

She curled up on the sofa, leaning on a stack of pillows. Almost as soon as she'd pulled the quilt around her shoulders, she quickly dozed off and did not wake until the next morning.

The house was quiet and still quiet. The TV's frozen screen offered options of 'Bonus Scenes' or the 'Story behind the Movie' both of which obviously had followed the end of the movie that she hadn't even seen.

Shaking her head, Claire laughed at herself slightly, remembering that Daniel had always teased her about never seeing an entire movie, but rather fallen asleep before the opening credits had even finished.

Tossing back her treasured quilt, Claire got up from the sofa, adjusted the thermostat, aware of the chill inside the house and went to the kitchen to pour herself a glass of orange juice.

Pulling out a stool at the short little bar counter, she saw the two, small boxes she'd left there, wrapped in cheerful holiday paper and remembered that it was Christmas morning. She'd been dreading the day. But, she'd promised Layne that she'd open her gifts.

Claire unwrapped the first box and found inside a beautiful silver and gold cross on a delicate chain. Also inside the box was a small imprinted card with her favorite poem imprinted on it, reminding her that '*when she saw only one set of footprints in the sand, it was then that God carried her.*'

"Layne," she said, smiling and remembering the day that she, herself, had told Layne to remember those encouraging words. And now, it was her daughter who was reminding Claire that she wasn't alone.

Opening the second gift, Claire found a six-inch long wine-colored velvet box with a matching satin bow. Thinking the beautiful box held a piece of jewelry, Claire lifted the top off of the box and saw inside a large silver heart-shaped ornament with a satin ribbon attached to a smaller silver heart. On the front of the larger heart, there was an inscription: "**In Our Hearts Forever.**"

Realizing that the biggest heart had a clasp, she opened it. Looking inside of the heart, Claire was met with a smiling photo of Daniel and her self, hugging and laughing with the pond behind the mountain house in the background. She immediately hugged the heart to her chest, closing her eyes for a moment. She saw that on the left side of the heart-shaped ornament, there was an inscription that read:

Daniel James Mitchell * A life well lived * A life well loved

Claire's heart warmed and flooded with love, both for Daniel and for her sweet children, who'd thought to give her such a treasured keepsake. She clutched the open heart to her chest again, closing her eyes and a single tear slid slowly down her cheek.

Uplifted by her children's special gifts, Claire decided she'd go for a walk and enjoy the cool, brisk Christmas morning. Sticking to the icy, dirt roads, where walking was easiest, Claire found herself passing the Wimbley's big farmhouse.

A large, festive wreath hung on their brick-red front door and a big cord of firewood was stacked neatly on their side porch.

"Merry Christmas, Claire!" she heard Mr. Wimbley call out as he came around the corner of his tidy house.

"Merry Christmas!" Claire replied, smiling and waving at the sight of her old friend who was making his way toward her, careful not to slip on his icy front walk.

Claire walked up and hugged him, always glad to see him.

"You have plans for supper today, Claire?" he asked.

"Truthfully, I haven't even thought about it," Claire answered honestly, feeling anything but in the holiday spirit.

"Well, it's settled then!" Mr. Wimbley said, his blue eyes twinkling. "You'll be *our* guest! Supper's at 6:00!"

"Oh, no! I couldn't possibly impose!" Claire protested.

"Nonsense, Girly!" he objected, smiling and putting up his weathered palm, before Claire could even finish speaking. "*Family* is never an imposition!"

"Well, then," Claire said, not wanting to offend the kind man, "What may I bring?"

"You just bring a good appetite, Claire!" he answered, taking in her slight figure. "Looks like you need a good meal!"

"I'll look forward to it!" Claire said, hugging Mr. Wimbley, then waving good-bye as she walked through his white wooden gate to resume her walk, buoyed by the old man's cheerful kindness.

Later, Claire drove into town, in hopes of finding at least a convenience store open on Christmas Day so she could pick up a few basic staples for her pantry. Pulling her car into the little Mountain-Mart store, she saw a man coming out carrying a bag of ice and realized the store must be open.

Wandering through the little store, Claire found a small selection of produce and was surprised even to find fresh cranberries. She decided to bake a loaf of her cranberry bread to take to the Wimbley's later that evening.

117

Back at her house, and grateful to have something to occupy her afternoon, Claire began preparing her cranberry bread, first cooking the berries in sugary water on the stovetop.

Later, while waiting for the fresh dough to rise twice, she thumbed through some architectural and decorating magazines that she'd brought along with her from Florida.

Hours later, after removing the two loaf pans from the old oven, Claire drizzled a sweet glaze across each plump loaf and left the bread to cool while she showered and dressed for supper.

Claire chose a mulberry-colored cowl necked sweater and tailored black Tahari slacks. Putting on her diamond stud earrings, she remembered that Daniel had surprised her with the earrings a couple of Christmases earlier.

She dried her hair and let it fall loosely over her shoulders, put on just a touch of makeup and chose a sensible pair of black flats, conscious that she'd have to walk up the Wimbley's icy front walk.

Looking at her reflection in the mirror, she desperately wished that she were dressing for Christmas dinner with Daniel.

Instead of dealing with her feelings of loneliness, Claire decided that she'd enjoy the evening with her old friends. She grabbed the bread loaves she'd wrapped and placed them in a basket, put on her black pea coat and headed toward the door.

Opening the outer storm door that led to the back porch, Claire saw that light snow flurries were gently dusting the cold, still yard. With her free hand, Claire tossed her the colorful wool scarf round her neck that always hung from her pea coat and she carefully made her way down the back steps and to her waiting SUV.

Chapter 14

Turning into the Wimbley's driveway, saw that Mr. Wimbley was already coming out to greet her, smiling as always. She realized he'd been watching for her from his front window.

Helping her, as she stepped down from her car, Mr. Wimbley gave her a long, tight hug.

"Hope you brought your appetite!" he said cheerfully, giving her a peck on the cheek. "The missus has been in that kitchen all day and she can't wait to see you!"

"I've brought an appetite *and* some warm cranberry bread!" Claire said, reaching into her car for the basket that sat on the passenger's seat.

"Now, you didn't have to go and do that!" he said.

"The *least* I could do!" Claire said, grateful to be included in the Wimbley's supper plans on Christmas.

"Well, come on in now!" Mr. Wimbley said, his hand on Claire's back, guiding her toward the steps of his side porch, "Bea is so happy you'll be here tonight!"

Stepping through the kitchen door, they found Mrs. Wimbley bent over and taking a turkey from her oven.

"Perfect timing!" she said in her sweet, singsong voice. Putting the turkey on her giant butcher-block island, she immediately hugged Claire tightly, still wearing her red oven mitts. "I'll just be a few minutes," she said, "Why don't you and James go and have a drink in the living room?"

"Oh, let me help you!" Claire insisted.

"I wouldn't think of it! You visit with James! I'll only be a few minutes!" Mrs. Wimbley said.

"Better come with me, Claire," Mr. Wimbley said, winking, "I've known the woman all my life and she's a stubborn one!"

"Mmmm, Claire! This bread smells heavenly!" Mrs. Wimbley said, as Claire started unbuttoning her coat, "We'll slice it with supper! Thank you, Dear!"

Mr. Wimbley held the swing door open that connected the farmhouse kitchen to the living room, so Claire could step through it ahead of him. As she stepped into the living room, Claire saw the back of a man's head who was seated on the sofa, just beyond the heavy oak dining table that was beautifully set for supper.

"Claire, this is Matt," Mr. Wimbley said, getting the attention of the man on the sofa. As the dark-haired man turned around, smiling, Claire gasped, instantly recognizing the other dinner guest.

"Oh, I think we've already met, James," the good-looking man answered, still smiling as Claire blushed, sputtering an awkward, "Ah, yes, hello, again."

"You know Matt already?" Mr. Wimbley asked, looking at Claire with a confused expression. "He's the handyman I recommended for your window problems," he went on.

"Oh, uh, we sort of ran into each other in my kitchen," Claire replied, remembering how embarrassed she'd been wearing only her towel in front of the stranger.

"Well, it's a pleasure to meet you formally," Matt said, offering his hand to Claire.

"Yes, you too," Claire replied, wanting to melt away, as she remembered her previous rudeness and embarrassment.

Thankfully, Mrs. Wimbley backed through the kitchen's swing door, at that very moment, carrying a huge platter. "Who *else* is starving?" she asked, prompting everyone to head to the table.

"May I take your coat for you?" Matt asked, reaching toward Claire's shoulders from behind her, causing her to flinch.

"Oh, oh, yes," Claire stammered, Thanks." In her embarrassment she hadn't even realized that she was still wearing her heavy coat and scarf.

"Well," Mr. Wimbley said, "We didn't get to have that drink yet! Who'd like some wine with dinner?" as he reached for an open bottle of Pinot Grigio on the sideboard behind the dining table.

"Perfect!" Claire said, relieved for the distraction, and feeling like she could use a few sips of wine at that moment.

Turning to sit down at the table, she jumped again slightly, as Matt pulled her chair out for her. "Oh! Thank you!" she said, still feeling as if she were wearing that yellow towel and nothing else.

Mr. Wimbley poured four glasses of wine, passed them around and then pulled out Bea's chair at the end of the table, after she'd placed the last serving bowl on the long dining table.

"Bea," he said, "Looks like you've done it *again*!" For *fifty-seven* Christmases now, I've eaten your wonderful Christmas suppers!"

He raised his wine glass, his blue eyes filled with love as he looked at Bea, "And I've looked at my beautiful love at this very table! To you, my love, the best Christmas gift I've ever received!"

"Here, here!" Matt said, raising his glass as they all toasted Mrs. Wimbley, who was feeling a bit embarrassed, but full of love for the sweet man at the opposite end of the table.

Claire took a sip of her wine, swallowing hard through the lump in her throat, aware that she wouldn't have any more Christmases with her own love. Fighting back the tears, she took a second sip, trying to push down the lump in her throat and willing the tears not to flow.

"This looks just wonderful!" Claire said, forcing a smile.

"White or dark?" Mr. Wimbley asked, as he carved the turkey.

"White, please," Claire answered, holding her plate closer to Mr. Wimbley, and grateful for anything that would keep her from having to look across the table and at the handsome man only a few feet away.

"Are you getting settled in over at the house, Claire?" Mrs. Wimbley asked as she passed a bowl of mashed sweet potatoes to Matt.

"Pretty much," Claire said. "I'm not in a huge hurry, really."

"Well, I'd be happy to take a look at those windows for you sometime!" Matt said, smiling at Claire.

"Yes," Claire said, forced now to look at him. "That'd be great."

Between the wine and her embarrassment over seeing Matt again, Claire again adjusted the neck of her sweater, feeling very warm and uncomfortable.

"Mrs. Wimbley, thanks for asking me to supper," Matt said, "You're an incredible cook!"

"Well, I love to cook for people who enjoy it!" the pretty, white-haired woman answered, smiling.

"Weren't you still at your sister's place last Christmas dealing with that illness you'd had?" Mr. Wimbley asked Matt.

"Yeah," Matt said. "That was a pretty tough time. For me **and** for her! She has young kids you know, so it was hard for her taking care of me till the doctors were able to able to fix me up again!"

"I never *did* know just what they did for you finally," Mr. Wimbley said to Matt.

"Oh a bunch of stuff," Matt said, "Not exactly supper table conversation though!"

Then, turning his attention to Claire, Matt asked, "So how long do you think you'll be in Virginia, Claire?"

"Oh, I haven't really decided for sure. I'm just taking it day by day."

"I think that sounds like a good plan, Dear!" Mrs. Wimbley said.

"Yep," Mr. Wimbley added. "Why rush things? And, you know we're here you, day or night, if you need anything, Claire."

"I *do* know that," Claire said, smiling. "And, I really appreciate you both more than you know."

An hour later, still seated at the dinner table, Mrs. Wimbley asked, "Well, anyone for warm apple pie?"

"You've twisted my arm, though I don't know where I'll put it!" Matt said, grinning. "But let me help you with these dishes first."

And he quickly stood up, stacked a few dishes and headed to the kitchen, with Claire doing the same.

"Now, you two go on into the living room!" Mrs. Wimbley insisted. "I'll do these later! You're company!"

At Mrs. Wimbley's insistence, Matt and Claire, reluctantly joined Mr. Wimbley in the living room where he was pouring four cups of coffee.

"Well, thank you," Claire said, as he handed her the light blue china cup on its delicate matching saucer.

"Here we are," Mrs. Wimbley said as she carried slices of her homemade apple pie atop her best silver tray into the living room. "The apples are from our trees out back!" she said, "I canned them earlier this year in the fall so I'd have them all winter!"

The small group of friends chatted easily for another hour or so in the Wimbley's cozy living room till Claire

said, "Well, I should probably be going,"
and she stood up.

"I'm so glad you came, Claire," Mrs.
Wimbley said, rising and hugging her
tightly, "It's been good visiting with you
again. But, don't you be a stranger now!"

"That's right!" Mr. Wimbley said.
"We're just down the road a bit! You stop
over any time at all! Kitchen door's
always open!"

"I'll do that!" Claire promised.

"Let me walk you out," Matt said,
squashing Claire's plans of making her
escape as quickly as she'd hoped.

Matt helped her to put on her coat,
held the front door open for her and told
the Wimbleys that he'd be right back
inside.

"Here you go," Matt said, putting his
left hand on Claire's elbow, and his right
hand in the small of her back, as she
stepped carefully down the Wimbley's front
steps that were just beginning to ice over
again.

"Ah, thank you," Claire said, feeling
a bit of an electric jolt race through her
body with Matt's touch.

Walking toward her SUV, Claire felt
uncomfortable with Matt, but due only to
her own rudeness when they'd met by
accident at her house previously.

"Matt, I want to apologize for - "
she started.

"No apology needed," he cut her off, smiling. "It was entirely my fault! But, yellow *is* a very good color on you!"

And he looked down and grinned that fabulous white grin at Claire that made her weak in the knees once again. As Claire reached for the door handle of her SUV, Matt quickly grabbed it first.

"Allow me," he said, opening the door, so Claire could step onto the running board and up into the SUV.

"Thank you," Claire said, appreciating Matt's gentlemanly gestures just as she'd always loved them in Daniel.

"Good night, Claire," Matt said, "Drive safely."

And he shut her door and waved as she backed slowly down the Wimbley's icy driveway with her heart pounding in her chest like a jackhammer.

Chapter 15

Over the next few days, Claire quietly busied herself around her house. For years, she and Daniel had talked about projects they'd like to accomplish around the old house, but between raising kids and running businesses, it seemed they'd never found the time.

Now though, Claire realized that she had nothing *but* time. She had made a list of all the things she wanted to do to the house. Paint; new floors; windows; drapes; cabinets; a new front door and a few other odds and ends made up her lengthy list.

Looking at her long list, Claire realized she'd need some help to accomplish some of her more difficult repairs. She reached for the copy of the small, local town newspaper on the nearby coffee table and found the 'Services' section where contractors listed their advertisements.

Her first call was a dead-end. "No, ma'am, I'm sorry," the man said, "But we're booked up through March." The second call yielded no answer at all. Claire's third call, however, was met with a familiar voice.

"Claire?" he said, "Is that *you?*"

Recognizing Matt's voice, Claire winced a bit, closing her eyes. "Um, yes, hi again, Matt!" she said, trying to sound relaxed and friendly.

"Small world!" he replied.

"I was looking for a painter when I called this number," Claire explained, "But I thought *you* did windows."

"Well, up here, we have to do a bit of everything!" he said. "So, I'm more of an all-around handyman, really."

"Oh, I see," Claire said, wondering how she could get out of talking with Matt about her painting needs because she felt so uncomfortable.

"So, you're also going to do some painting at your place?" Matt said to fill the awkward silence.

"Well, ah, yes," Claire replied, assuming Matt was envisioning her standing in front of him in her yellow towel.

"Great!" he said, "But, if you want it done any time soon, I hope you're thinking about painting only the *interior* of the house now."

"Oh, well, yes, of course," Claire said, feeling foolish for not thinking that it was freezing outside, making it impossible to work on the exterior yet.

"Why don't I stop out tomorrow and we can talk about what you need?" Matt asked.

"Oh, ah, yes! Sure!" Claire said, hesitantly, as she squeezed her eyes shut. "That sounds just great!"

Matt arrived early the next day, clipboard and tape measure in hand.

"Good morning!" he said, as Claire held open the back door for him.

"Hi, Matt," Claire said, nervous yet again, in Matt's presence, but unsure why. "Would you like some coffee?" she offered.

"Oh, no, thanks! Already had two cups!" Matt said, looking around the kitchen.

"Okay, then," Claire said nervously, setting down her own coffee mug on the counter. "Let me show you around."

As she turned to lead Matt through the kitchen and into the living room, Matt couldn't help but notice the subtle scent of her perfume.

"I'm thinking of using cottage-style colors throughout the house," she began.

Matt laughed slightly, catching her off guard. "You *must* be an interior decorator! You've got to make it simple for us, country guys!"

"Well, yes, I'm a designer, actually," Claire said, also laughing. "Guess it shows, huh?"

"You'll have to be patient with me!" Matt said, "I'm used to white, off-white and tan! Nothin' too fancy!"

"Don't worry," Claire assured him, "I'll spec-out the job for you, giving you exact selections, with color names and numbers."

Claire was feeling a bit more relaxed and in control again as she and Matt continued to discuss her plans for the house.

After they'd walked through both floors of the entire house, Matt said, "I think you can keep me busy for a long time!"

"I know it's a lot of work," Claire said, "But I'm really in no hurry."

"Well, I could use the work to be honest," Matt told her. "I wasn't able to work till recently."

"Yes, I heard Mr. Wimbley mention you'd been ill," Claire said. "What happened?"

"Now that's a long and boring story!" Matt said, hoping to change the subject.

Sensing his need for privacy, Claire said, "Well, I'm glad to see you're doing better now!"

"Thanks, and I'll have a complete estimate to you by tomorrow!" Matt said, as he headed out the back door.

Claire was thrilled to hear Elaine's voice on the phone later that day.

"So, how are things going up there?" Elaine asked.

"Not bad," Claire answered. "I'm keeping busy, and I've decided to work on the house and spruce it up finally."

"You know, I'd always wondered how Dan ended up with that house in the first place," Elaine said. "I'd have thought it would have gone to his oldest brother."

"Daniel's parents had put it in their will that he'd get the house because he'd always loved it as a boy. They knew he'd keep it in the family, I think," Claire explained. "And his brothers each got a nice cash inheritance instead, which suited everyone at the time."

"Hmm," Elaine said. "I'd always been curious about that."

"Well, I'm just so glad to have this place now!" Claire told her. "And Danny and Layne can bring their own children here one day, which would make Daniel so happy!"

"You're right!" Elaine agreed. "But, what about you, Claire? Aren't you lonely up there?"

"Heavens, no!" Claire said. "But if you'd like to come up, the door's always open."

"I *would* like to visit, actually," Elaine said.

"If you want to fly up, I can pick you up in Roanoke," Claire went on, "I know how you hate to drive!"

"So *right* you are, my friend!" Elaine said. "I'll make a reservation and get the info to you! Can't wait!"

———————

Chapter 16

Two weeks later, Claire was turning into the Roanoke Airport, eager to see her oldest and dearest friend. Only minutes later, she and Elaine were rushing to hug each other inside the small airport.

"Claire!" Elaine said, grinning as she dropped her suitcase to hug Claire. "You're starting to look like your old self again!" she said.

"Oh no! That bad, huh?" Claire joked as she reached for Elaine's bag. "I'm parked close!" she went on, "Then we have about an hour's drive up to the house!"

A short while later, Claire pulled the SUV up the gravel path that led to the mountain house. Seeing the pick-up truck parked outside Claire's house, Elaine asked, "Hey, who's at your house?"

"Oh, that's Matt's truck," Claire explained. "He's the painter I told you about."

Claire parked next to Matt's big, red truck, then helped Elaine get her bags from the back of the SUV.

Pushing open the back door and stepping inside the kitchen, Elaine caught sight of a shirtless, very muscular man in jeans, atop a ladder, with his back toward the women.

"Oh, Lordy!" Elaine exclaimed aloud appreciating the sight.

Startled, Matt backed down the ladder and quickly grabbed his shirt from a nearby chair. Slipping into the shirt, he buttoned it, and then turned around toward the women.

"Sorry, ladies!" he said. "I wasn't expecting you back so soon and I got a bit warm in here while I was working!"

"I'll say! It's definitely *hot* in here!" Elaine said, obviously appreciating Matt's muscular build.

Matt turned toward Claire, looking noticeably uncomfortable. Trying to change the subject, he said, "I hope the paint smell won't bother you, ladies, too much tonight."

"Oh, no!" Claire assured him. "And, Matt, this is my friend, Elaine."

Matt shook Elaine's hand. "Nice to meet you, Elaine. Here, let me take those bags upstairs for you, ladies," he said, reaching for her suitcases, before either woman could object.

When he'd gone up the stairs, Elaine rolled her eyes and whispered, "Good Lord! He is beyond gorgeous! Do *all* the mountain men look like that up here?"

"Elaine, might I remind you that you're a happily married woman?" Claire reminded her friend.

"Yes, but I am also an art lover, Claire! I can appreciate fine art, even if

I don't collect it!" Elaine whispered, "And THAT is definitely a fine work of art!"

Matt stepped back into the kitchen. "Claire, I think I'll clean-up for today and let you and Elaine visit. I'll be back in the morning though."

"Sounds great!" Claire said, as Elaine's eyes pleaded with her to have Matt stay longer.

For the next week, Claire and Elaine visited, talked, laughed and cried together. They took long walks and stayed up till the wee hours of the morning each day, talking sometimes nearly till dawn.

One night, while they were sitting in the rockers on the porch, Elaine said, "Claire, you know it's been nearly a year now."

"Trust me, El, I know how long it's been!" Claire said, "If *anyone* knows, I do!"

"Well," Elaine continued slowly, "Have you noticed that the drop-dead, gorgeous man who visits you daily, seems to be very interested in you?"

"El, you know I love Daniel!" Claire said defensively.

"Yes, Hon," Elaine continued, "But, you, my friend, have the rest of your life ahead of you!"

"I'd never betray Daniel! Never!" Claire said, shocked that Elaine would even suggest that she date another man.

"Dan wants you to be happy, Claire! He expects you to find love again!"

"I've found love! I'm IN love with my *husband*! With Daniel!" Claire went on, "Why do you want me to move on when I'm not ready? I may never be ready!"

"I know Claire," Elaine said. "Calm down. I'm not trying to upset you, really."

The two friends rocked silently, looking at the stars. "I'm scared, El," Claire said finally.

"I know," Elaine said, putting her hand on Claire's. "I'm not asking you to commit to an intense relationship with this guy. Just be open to a new friendship, that's all."

Chapter 17

Claire and Elaine had just gotten out of bed when Matt arrived. "Good morning, ladies!" he said. "My sister sent these over for you."

Claire looked inside the paper bag that Matt handed to her. "Hot, fresh donuts! How sweet of her!" she exclaimed.

"Annie and her husband own the little cafe' in town and twice a week she makes fresh donuts. She thought you two would enjoy them."

"Well, please thank her for us!" Claire said. "This is such a nice treat!"

"Will do!" Matt said. "Oh, and Claire, when you get time, I think we should talk about plumbing. I was looking in the basement and under the house, and you may want to think about re-plumbing the place before there's a problem."

"Okay," Claire answered. "Elaine has to leave tomorrow, so I'll be free then."

The next day, Claire drove Elaine back to the airport in Roanoke. "Claire, will you give it a chance?" Elaine asked.

"What?" Claire asked quizzically, "Give *what* a chance?"

"Matt!" Elaine said, obviously exasperated with her friend. "Will you give it a chance with *Matt*?" Hugging her friend a last time, Claire said, "No promises, El! But, I do enjoy talking with him."

"I'll take that as a *yes!*" Elaine said, tossing her big purse over her shoulder, and then waving to Claire as she headed toward the gate at the airport.

Back at her house again, Claire and Matt talked over Matt's recommendations for new pipes throughout the house. "With all you're doing," he went on, "You might want to consider it. The plumbing is ancient in this place."

"Daniel had mentioned that before, too," Claire said, "But we never got around to it. Go ahead, Matt, whatever you think. I trust your judgment."

"I wouldn't steer you wrong, Claire," he said, looking into Claire's green eyes. Uncomfortable, Claire averted her eyes, reached for a nearby dishtowel, and began wiping the counters, nervously, with her back to Matt.

"Oh!" she went on, "And, by the way, the paint job looks great!"

"Thanks! I really like the colors you picked," Matt said. "You're obviously really good at what you do!"

"I enjoy decorating," Claire said, polishing the faucet at the sink, "But I haven't worked since…"

"I know," Matt said. "I'm sorry about your husband, Claire. The Wimbleys told me all about him and what a great guy he was."

Suddenly, Claire felt Matt's hand on her shoulder. "Ah, thank you," she answered nervously. "It's been a rough time."

"I understand," he said, removing his hand. "Uh, Claire," he said, "I was wondering if you might like to have dinner one night."

"Oh, I don't know," she began, "I don't think…"

"It's just dinner," Matt said. "Just two new friends having dinner and talking. That's it."

"Matt, I don't think…" she began.

"Claire, I hope you won't shoot me down," he grinned, "It was really hard for me to get up the courage to ask you! It's been a while since I've asked out a beautiful woman!"

Smiling, Claire said, "Okay, then, yes, dinner would be nice."

Relieved that she'd accepted his invitation, Matt again placed his hand on her arm. "Great! Tomorrow night, then? Seven o'clock?"

"Oh, ah, sure," Claire said, still wondering if she was doing the right thing.

"I'll be here to pick you up at seven then!" Matt said, smiling.

"Oh, I can just meet you somewhere," Claire began.

"Are you kidding?" Matt said, "What kind of guy would I be to let you meet me at the restaurant? We, country boys, DO have manners! I'll be here for you tomorrow night at seven!"

As Matt left, Claire watched his truck back down her gravel path. She waved and smiled, then sat down on her back steps.

Looking out, across the pond, she said, "Oh, Daniel."

For the rest of the evening, Claire wrestled with her feelings and inner turmoil, not knowing if she should have dinner with Matt or not. She slept fitfully that night, warmed by her favorite quilt.

The next morning, she awoke to sunlight streaming into her bedroom. She lingered in bed, longer than usual, thinking of Daniel. *And thinking of Matt.*

Realizing that she was thinking of Matt, Claire silently chastised herself for thinking of anyone other than her beloved Daniel.

"Oh, Daniel," she whispered, "I'm sorry. I don't know what to do."

Feeling exhausted from her restless night, Claire got up, slipped into her sweats and twisted her shiny ponytail into a bun, securing it atop her head. Matt had said he wouldn't be working on the house that day, because he needed to pick-up more supplies, but that he'd see her for dinner.

After straightening her bed, Claire grabbed a basket of her dirty laundry and headed down to the basement, carefully navigating the steep wooded steps. At the base of the steps, Claire turned and set the basket on the dryer beneath the steps.

Absent-mindedly separating her dark and light clothes, Claire happened to look up and noticed the carving on the back of one of the open steps. It had been carved there decades earlier. She smiled, remembering the day that Daniel had carved the words: "*Daniel & Claire Forever.*"

Claire reached up, standing on her toes, to trace the letters now, thinking about that day, when she and Daniel had been carefree college students.

*

Daniel had brought Claire home to meet his parents, eager to show-off the long-legged beauty who'd almost instantly captured his heart. His parents immediately had adored Claire and were thrilled to see their son so happy.

One afternoon, Claire had asked Mrs. Mitchell if she could do some laundry. "I'll show you where the washer is," Daniel said, holding the basement door open for Claire.

As soon as Claire had started the washer, Daniel spun her around and kissed her passionately for what seemed like

forever, to Claire, as she melted into Daniel.

Then, reaching into his jeans pocket, Daniel found a pocketknife and carved the words into the wood above the washer.

"Your mom is going to kill you!" Claire told him.

"Not as soon as she hears that you're going to be Mrs. Daniel Mitchell! And that we will be presenting her with some new, little Mitchells before long!"

And with that, Daniel kissed Claire again.

*

Snapped back into reality by the sound of the phone ringing upstairs, Claire took a deep breath and switched off the light above the washer.

"Hello?" she answered, out of breath from running up the stairs.

"Mom?" Layne said. "You okay?"

"Hi, Hon!" Claire said, thrilled to hear her daughter's voice.

"Yes, I'm fine. I was just doing some laundry downstairs."

"Well, I was just calling to see how you're doing," Layne said.

"I'm doing much better," her mom told her, "But what about you and Danny? How are you two?"

"We're good," Layne said. "Just swamped with classes and we're both seeing new people, so things are really good here."

"Did you get the Snickerdoodle cookies I sent?" Claire asked.

"Oh, yeah!" Layne said. "Thanks!"

Claire enjoyed catching-up with her daughter, learning all about Layne's new boyfriend and what she'd been up to lately. Hearing Layne talk reminded Claire of when she and Daniel had met. She could hear the excitement in her daughter's voice as she spoke about her new guy.

"But, Mom," Layne added, "What about *you*?"

"What do you mean?" Claire asked.

"What's new with *you*? Are you lonely up there?"

"What? No!" Claire assured her. "In fact, it's been just what I needed. To be up here, working on the house, relaxing, doing whatever I want."

Claire realized that she'd stopped just short of telling Layne about Matt. She didn't know how Layne would feel about her mom having dinner with a man.

"Well, Mom, we love you!" Layne said, after they'd talked for nearly an hour.

"Love you guys, too!" Claire said, feeling a bit guilty for not mentioning that she was planning to have dinner with Matt.

'*But, we're just friends*,' she thought to herself.

Hanging up the phone in it's cradle on the wall, Claire looked down at her wedding rings. She hadn't removed her rings in over two decades. And she'd worn the third diamond band that Daniel had given her since their tenth wedding anniversary.

Fingering the rings, she clutched her left hand to her chest. "Oh, Daniel," she whispered, closing her eyes, "Tell me what to do!"

Seconds later, with a heavy heart, Claire opened her eyes, surprised to see a tiny, brilliant red bird on the windowsill outside the kitchen window. The little bird was just standing at the window, looking at her, and cocking his head, side to side.

"Well, hello there, Little One!" Claire said, smiling. "You're a welcome sight! Spring has definitely sprung, I guess!" And with that, the bird turned and flew away.

Claire stepped toward the window to watch the little bird as he soared over the treetops and out of her sight.

Chapter 18

Later that afternoon, Claire realized that she was feeling a bit nervous about being with Matt later that evening. She realized, though, that she also felt a twinge of excitement, almost like a teenager, anticipating a first date once again.

Her mix of emotions had her stomach in knots and she made herself a cup of chamomile tea to settle it. Sipping her tea, she wandered into her bedroom to figure out what she'd wear that night.

Standing in the closet, surveying her hanging clothes, Claire's eyes fell on the 'the white box' atop a shelf that was eye-level to her, reminding her that it was time she made plans to spread Daniel's ashes.

She touched the side of the box and stepped from the closet, torn between her aching love for Daniel and her desperate need to heal her heart.

Getting ready later, Claire enjoyed a hot shower leisurely taking her time till the hot water abruptly ran out. *'Definitely need to get a bigger hot water heater when we re-do that plumbing,'* she thought, reminded of Matt's suggestion.

Stepping from the cast iron tub, Claire saw her reflection in the mirror over the pedestal sink.

*'What are you **doing**, Claire?'* she thought silently, also wondering if she should phone Matt to cancel for the evening. Looking at her watch lying on the nearby hamper, she realized Matt would arrive in a little over an hour. *'No,'* she thought, *'That would be so rude.'*

Nearly an hour later, Claire stood in front of the full-length mirror in her bedroom. She'd chosen a green off-the-shoulder mohair sweater with a wide brown leather belt. The sweater flattered her figure as it hung over her tan slacks. The green shade was stunning next to her shiny auburn hair that hung past her shoulders, just barely touching the top of the sweater.

Reaching down to zip the inside of her short boot, Claire heard a car coming up the path, slowly rolling over the gravel. Suddenly, her stomach knotted, as she realized 'her date' was arriving.

Nervously, Claire took one last glance in the mirror, and then grabbed her purse and headed to get her coat from the closet near the door. Matt was already knocking on the door.

Her long black wool coat in-hand, Claire opened the heavy door, having to tug a bit, as it stuck in the doorframe, as always.

"Well, hello there!" Matt said, grinning.

"Oh! Hi!" Claire said nervously.

"Wow! You look extraordinary!" he said honestly, surveying Claire appreciatively.

"Well, thank you!" she said, avoiding eye contact and feeling a bit awkward, as she started to put on her coat.

"Here, allow me," Matt said as he reached for the coat and lifted it up and over Claire's shoulders. As she lifted her hair from the back of the coat, Matt caught the scent of her perfume mixed with her shampoo. Not wanting to make her even more uncomfortable, though, he didn't mention how incredible she smelled, but rather he just silently soaked-in her incredible scent.

"Hungry?" he asked.

"I am!" Claire answered, realizing she was feeling warm and flushed at the moment.

"Good, because we're going to a little place one town over that has fabulous food," Matt told her, as they both walked outside.

Matt opened Claire's door and she climbed up and into the high truck into the passenger's seat. As he got into his seat, she exclaimed, "Ok, how do you keep your truck so clean up here in the mountains with all the dirt roads?"

"Just washed her today!" he said grinning, "Wouldn't want to pick-up a beautiful lady in a dirty truck, now would I?"

A few minutes later, while they were driving, Claire realized she was actually feeling at ease, talking easily with Matt, as he drove along the winding mountain roads.

"So, are you originally from this area?" she asked.

"Oh, no," he said, "I grew up in Charleston actually. A couple years back, though, my sister and her husband came up here when he got transferred with his company to oversee the logging outfit in town."

"So, how did *you* end up here?" Claire persisted.

"Well now, that's a long story," Matt explained. "I got sick and my sister asked me to come up here so she could help me out and still care for her family. Then, I had a medical procedure at Duke, about three hours away, and Annie offered to continue to look after me while I recuperated."

Claire felt like she was prying. "Well, you couldn't have picked a more beautiful area!" she said, realizing Matt wanted to keep things to himself obviously.

"Yeah, I love it up here!" he said. Changing the subject, Matt said, "I hear you have two great kids!"

"Now, how'd you hear about Layne and Danny?" Claire asked.

"Well, the Wimbleys mentioned them and also your friend, Elaine, talked about them when she was here," he explained. "She said your family's been coming up here for years."

Wondering what else Elaine had chatted with Matt about, Claire said, "Once or twice a year for over twenty years actually. We all love it up here!"

The easy conversation continued for another few minutes as they neared the little restaurant. "Here we are!" Matt said turning his truck into the parking lot of a quaint little restaurant set back from the road.

"Bluebells," Claire said reading the wooden sign out front. "Is this place new?" she asked, "I don't remember it."

"Not really," he said, "But this past winter was the first winter it's been open. The fall season is really their busy-time, when the leaves change and all the tourists come up."

"I'll bet!" Claire said, remembering the postcard-perfect foliage the area offered during the fall months.

Stepping into the quaint little restaurant, Claire and Matt were greeted by an older woman who obviously knew Matt. Hugging him, she looked around his tall frame toward Claire. "Hi there!" she said, "I'm Catherine!" She offered her hand to Claire.

"Nice to meet, you Catherine," Claire said, smiling, and shaking hands.

"I have a table for you two over near the fireplace!" Catherine said, reaching for two menus from the wall pocket beside her.

"Perfect!" Claire said, noticing all the carefully displayed antiques and collectibles in the cozy restaurant, as Matt guided her to follow Catherine.

"Here we are!" Catherine said, indicating a small table beside a raised brick fireplace near the back of the restaurant, "And, I'll take your coats for you so you can get comfortable!"

As Catherine walked away with their coats, Matt pulled out Claire's chair for her, and then took his seat, opposite her. The raised fireplace hearth was at just about the same height as their table.

"What a great little place!" Claire said, noticing about a half-dozen other couples at nearby tables in the small place.

"Catherine is the owner," Matt told her. "She's also my sister's neighbor. She's more like an aunt to Annie's kids, really."

"I can tell she really enjoys owning this place," Claire said. "So, what's good?" she said, opening her tall menu.

"Literally, everything!" Matt said. "I'm serious! Most of the dishes are Catherine's family's recipes. Best food around here!"

Suddenly, Catherine appeared again, carrying a wine bottle. "Compliments of the house!" she said, pouring red wine first into Claire's glass, and then into Matt's.

"Well, thank you!" Matt said.

"It's good to see you smiling, Matt!" Catherine said to Matt, winking at him. "You two go over the menus and I'll be back in a few!"

"To new friends!" Matt said, raising his glass to Claire.

"New friends!" Claire said, smiling as she raised her glass to Matt's. Taking a drink, Claire said, "This wine is fantastic!"

"From the winery up the road," Matt told her.

"Oh, yeah, I know it. Daniel and I went there…" Claire's voiced trailed off, as she looked away.

"It's okay, Claire," Matt said, placing his hand atop Claire's which was on the tabletop.

"I'm sorry," Claire said, shaking her head. "It's just that…"

"No apologies needed," Matt said, patting her hand. "Daniel was a lucky man, and I'm sure he knew it!"

"Thank you," Claire said, swallowing hard.

"Hey, those green eyes are much too beautiful to hold a second of sadness," Matt said honestly.

"Oh, Matt," Claire said, "You're so kind… I, just, I don't want to give you the wrong idea."

"The wrong idea?" Matt said, removing his hand and smiling. "I only have an idea that we're two new friends about to enjoy a delicious dinner together."

Smiling and relaxing a bit, Claire said, "Okay, thank you."

For the next two hours, Claire and Matt talked easily, feasting on baked Brie, venison and Crème Brulee.

Pouring the last of the wine into Claire's glass, Matt said, "I don't know if I've ever had a more enjoyable evening – *or* better company."

"This was just what I needed," Claire said, feeling slightly tipsy, but more relaxed than she could remember, "Thank you!"

"My pleasure," Matt replied, mesmerized by the reflection of the flames flickering in Claire's eyes in a way he knew he couldn't ignore for long.

Paying the check, Matt thanked Catherine and hugged her as she handed him their coats. Helping Claire with her coat, Matt was physically fighting an overwhelming urge to kiss the nape of her neck, when she pulled her shiny hair from the coat's collar.

When Claire reached for the doorknob, Matt was grateful for the rush of cool air in his face that helped him to re-focus.

The drive back to Claire's house was slow, as thick fog had blanketed the mountainous roads. Turning onto the gravel road to Claire's house, Matt said, "Well, Claire, I hope we'll do this again sometime."

"I do too!" Claire said, realizing that she meant it.

Matt walked Claire to her door, leaving his truck engine running, so knew he didn't expect to come inside.

"Thank you, again!" Claire said, feeling a bit awkward as she turned the key in her lock.

"The pleasure was all mine," Matt said, smiling. "And, I'll be by in the morning to get some more work done!"

"Great!" Claire said, feeling a bit like an awkward schoolgirl as she stood inside the doorway of her house. "Good night!" And she went inside quickly and closed the door.

Chapter 19

Waking early the next morning, Claire phoned Elaine. "Tell me all about it!" Elaine said, "Every detail!"

After getting a play-by-play of the previous evening, Elaine said, "Claire, remember your promise!"

"What promise?" Claire asked innocently.

"You promised me that you'd keep an open mind."

"Oh… that…" Claire said.

"Yes, THAT!" Elaine said, "Claire, you're not a nun! Look around! You're not living in a convent up there! Life's too short!"

"You're telling *me*?" Claire said, referring to Daniel's life that was cut short all too soon.

"Well, you know what I'm saying!" Elaine persisted. "Just give it a chance, Claire. Have I ever given you bad advice?"

"I think you just want to live vicariously through me, El!" Claire said, smiling now.

"Yes, well, *that* too!" Elaine told her, laughing.

Shortly after hanging up the phone, Claire saw Matt's red truck pulling into the yard. Her heart raced, as she realized she was excited and pleased to see him again.

"Well, good morning, pretty lady!" he called as he walked up her back steps and she met him at the door.

"Good morning!" Claire said, smiling. "Coffee for you today?"

"No, thanks, I'd better get to work," he said, reaching past Claire for the ladder he'd left leaning in her kitchen. She could smell his cologne slightly and wondered if he'd always worn it while he was working.

While Matt worked installing more windows in the house, Claire sorted through the fabric swatches she'd selected. Sitting at her kitchen table, she looked up to see Matt come inside.

"Mind if I get a drink?" he asked, wiping his brow.

"Of course!" Claire said getting up from her chair. "Iced tea okay?"

"Great," Matt said, "It's definitely warming up a bit!"

"I know it!" Claire said as she poured the tea from a green, glass pitcher she'd retrieved from the refrigerator. "In fact, just the other day I saw the most beautiful little red bird right here by the window. My first sign of spring!"

"I think he's adopted us then," Matt said, laughing, "There's been a little red bird flying around all morning and he's so

160

comfortable that he even lands right where I'm working. You don't see that much."

"Here," Claire said, handing Matt the glass. "Why don't you sit down for a few minutes and take a break?"

"What's all this?" he asked, referring to Claire's fabric swatches and catalogs on the kitchen table.

"Oh! Let me show you!" she said. "These are the fabrics I'm using for the window coverings and I've also ordered a few new area rugs. Thought I'd add a bit more color in here!"

Sitting down in a chair at the table, Matt pulled a catalog closer to him, looking at more of Claire's selections. "Claire, you must be **some** kinda decorator back in Florida," he said. "You're really good! I'm lucky if I can match my shirt to my pants every morning!"

"Oh, it's just something that I really love doing," Claire said, appreciating that she had someone to share her plans with. "It's been a long time since I've sewn anything, but when the fabrics arrive, I plan to try my hand at making the window coverings myself. Daniel's mother's old sewing machine is upstairs still."

"So, you don't make the drapes for your clients then?" Matt asked.

"Oh, no!" Claire said, "We use **real** seamstresses for that! But, I sewed our drapes when Daniel and I were first married. And for the kids' rooms when they were little. It was more out of necessity back then, believe me!"

"You're really a take-charge woman, Claire!" Matt said, "I'll bet you can do whatever you set your mind to!"

"My friends refer to that as pure stubbornness!" Claire laughed, still appreciating the compliment.

For the next few days, Matt showed up like clockwork, working each day till sunset. One afternoon, Claire walked outside to survey his progress and found him at the top of a ladder he'd leaned against the house. Rounding the corner of the house, Claire saw him on the tall ladder, shirtless, in denim jeans, with his chiseled, muscular back toward her. Arms overheard, he was installing trim around an upstairs window.

Claire stopped and quietly watched as Matt's tanned muscles moved and flexed in his back and his upper arms, as he fitted the piece of trim at the sill and used a nail gun to secure it.

"Hey, there!" she called, realizing that he'd seen her standing nearby.

Matt looked over his shoulder, arms still overhead, "How's it look, Boss?"

Thankful that Elaine was not with her at that moment, Claire said, "You're doing a great job! I was wondering if you'd like something to eat for lunch?"

"Sure!" he called, "I'll need about fifteen minutes though."

"I'll meet you in the kitchen," she said, going back inside the house.

Later, as they ate lunch together, Matt said, "This is delicious, Claire! I swear I don't even know the last time I've had a beautiful woman cook for me!"

"Now, I don't believe that for even a minute!" Claire said, taking a bite of the chicken quesadilla from her own plate.

"No, really!" he went on, "It's been a long time."

"Well, I've really enjoyed having the company around here," Claire told him. "I'm actually going to miss having you here when you've finished all the repairs."

"Me, too," Matt said, looking seriously into Claire's eyes, until she pulled her gaze away uncomfortably. "So, Claire," he said, "Tell me about where you're from in Florida."

For the next half-hour, Claire told Matt all about how she and Daniel had bought their house as a fixer-upper, then done the renovations, little by little, as they could afford them, on their old house. She told him how it had been the perfect place to raise Danny and Layne. She talked of the family holidays they'd all cherished. And how she'd always loved going home to the big, old house.

"But, now," she went on, looking down, "It's just not the same."

"Well, what are you going to do with your house now?" Matt asked, "I mean, it *sounds* like it's a **lot** of house for one person."

"I know," she answered," But I just can't see myself selling it either! The memories ~ there are just so many!"

"Well," Matt said, "Had you and Dan planned to stay there after you'd both eventually retired?"

"He always said we'd sell it and downsize," Claire explained, "But, I'd always had this romantic notion of turning it into a grand bed and breakfast."

"I've always heard that a B&B is a LOT of work!" Matt laughed, raising his eyebrows.

"I know," Claire answered, "But I had visions of personally tending to my guests, providing a tea service every afternoon and a homemade breakfast every morning. And, I had all these great plans for decorating it, of course."

Looking around, Matt said, "Claire! That's it! I've got it!"

"Got what?" Claire said, both puzzled and startled by Matt's enthusiasm.

"Do it HERE!" he said, "Make THIS place a bed and breakfast!"

"What?" Claire said, looking around the small kitchen with its simplistic style.

"Think of it, Claire!" Matt went on. "This area is absolutely *booming* in the fall when the leaves change! You could just run your B&B seasonally, then take time off when the weather gets cold."

"Oh, I don't know … " Claire's voice trailed off, "This house is so small!"

"Uh, I do know of a pretty good handyman I could recommend to put on an addition for you! And he really needs the work, so he's not too expensive either!" Matt joked.

"You're serious, aren't you?" Claire said slowly.

"As a *heart attack*," Matt said. "This place would be perfect, Claire! Look at the scenery outside! It's perfect! The lake ~ the mountains all around ~ a few deer running through the backyard now and then."

"Hmmmm," Claire murmured, pondering the suggestion. "You're either on to something or you've absolutely lost your mind completely! But, I'll think on it."

Chapter 20

Days later, as Matt scraped loose, peeling paint from the exterior boards on Claire's house she drove into town for groceries. Driving along the winding road, she noticed a little wooden sign. *'Willows B&B'* it read.

Without another thought, Claire turned off the road and followed the additional signs to a quaint two-story home overlooking a picturesque rolling valley. Stopping her SUV, Claire surveyed the grounds of the cozy inn that appeared to still be closed, as it was still early in the year. The older home had white sideboards with wedgewood blue shutters and matching trim and a glass storm door protecting a heavy white door on the front of the home.

Trees surrounded the home, some of them with new buds promising glorious springtime blooms. A white gazebo sat beside the home with a bare trellis that Claire presumed held blossoming vines in warmer months. A stone path led from the front door round the side of the home and Claire imagined that countless couples had wandered down the path, hand-in-hand, to sit under the gazebo and look out over the picturesque scenery.

The deep front porch of the home had a worn, wooden floor, and Claire envisioned couples sitting on the porch sipping coffee and chatting about their plans for the day as the innkeeper set out homemade breakfasts for her guests inside.

Claire could see *herself* as that innkeeper, bustling about inside, wearing an apron, chatting with her guests and pouring them more coffee as they enjoyed her homemade muffins.

'*He's right!*' Claire thought, '*My house really does have the potential!*'

Smiling to herself, Claire put her SUV in reverse and backed down the path in front of the quiet home. Not taking her eyes off the road, Claire reached into her purse and felt around for her cell phone. Feeling it, she automatically pushed a button on it to see if she had service.

"Great! No bars!" she said to no one in particular, as she tossed the phone on the seat beside her.

A few miles later, as she drove closer to town, Claire heard a welcome chirp and realized she had cell phone service once again. She pulled her car over onto the shoulder of the road not wanting to move beyond the spot where she'd gotten a signal.

Seconds later, she heard Elaine's voice. "El?" she said excitedly, "Hey! It's Claire!"

"*You* sound excited! Calling to tell me you've taken my advice and let our favorite hunk sweep you off your feet?" Elaine laughed.

"Ah, no," Claire said, smiling and shaking her head at her relentless friend's comment. "But I *do* have news!"

"I'm sitting down," Elaine said, "Go ahead."

"You are speaking to the owner of the newest bed and breakfast up here in the mountains!" Claire said matter-of-factly.

Claire's announcement was met with dead silence.

"El?" she said, looking at her phone, "Hey? Did I lose you?"

"No, I'm here," Elaine said, "But you've *lost* your *mind*!"

"No! I'm serious!" Claire told her friend, "I really want to do this! You know I'd always wanted to make our Florida home a B&B one day. Why not do it up *here*?"

"Claire, do you have any idea of the work involved in that kind of business?" Elaine said, obviously shocked at Claire's announcement.

"El, I have the perfect place for it!" Claire went on. "I mean, my house isn't big, but it's got such potential! And it'd give me such satisfaction!"

"Why would you want to work yourself like a dog, day in and day out?" Elaine

169

asked. "You obviously don't need the money, Claire. I don't get it!"

"True," Claire agreed. "But you know how I love to have a project! And this would keep me busy!"

"What about your place down here in Florida?" Elaine asked. "Are you not coming back here?"

"I don't know, really," Claire said thoughtfully, "But I don't have to decide that right now."

"Well then, what can I do to help you?" Elaine asked.

"Not a thing!" Claire told her. "If you'd just keep sending my mail up here every week or two, so I can stay on top of things, that'd be great!"

"Will do," Elaine said. "In fact I've got a big envelope of mail to send to you now. I dropped by your house yesterday and all was well."

"You're the best!" Claire said, smiling. "I'll let you know what's going on up here! Bye!"

Chapter 21

Returning to her house, Claire was disappointed to see that Matt's truck was already gone from her yard. He'd obviously finished for the day, Claire realized, and she was deflated not to have anyone to talk to about her new venture.

After putting away the last of her groceries, she realized the sun would be setting over the mountaintop in a little over an hour. There was something she'd been putting off and knew she could ignore it no longer.

As she walked into her bedroom, Claire picked up the framed photo of Daniel from her nightstand beside the bed. "Help me now, Daniel. Help me to be strong," she said, and then held the frame to her chest for a moment.

Minutes later, Claire was carrying the white box with her beloved's ashes as she walked along the rocky path behind her home. Looking around, she wasn't sure exactly where she'd take Daniel's ashes. And then, she remembered.

*

It had been a perfect fall day. Daniel had waked her up early nuzzling her neck and pulled her close.

"How 'bout a picnic today, Hon?" he said.

"Oh, yeah, the kids will love that!" Claire answered, trying to rub the sleep from her eyes.

"No, no," Daniel said, playfully kissing her, "Mrs. Wimbley asked if the kids could go over and bake with her today, remember? Just us. Just the two of us. What do you say?"

"That sounds perfect," Claire said, rolling over to cuddle Daniel, grateful that he always seized an opportunity for the two of them to spend time together.

Later that afternoon while Mrs. Wimbley watched Layne and Danny, Claire and Daniel took a backpack and a blanket and hiked through the woods near their house. They chatted happily, holding hands, as they hiked through the trees, up and over a pasture, alongside a stream and to a secluded scenic overlook.

Daniel spread their blanket in a partially shaded spot beneath a huge tree. It was a clear day with nothing but blue sky and glorious rolling red, orange and gold colors as far as the eye could see.

"Incredible," Claire said, her hands on her hips as she stood looking out across the valley below.

"This has always been my favorite spot up here," Daniel said, coming up behind her and wrapping his arms around her.

*

Claire realized that she was out of breath after hiking uphill for so long, carrying the box, and lost in her memories. But she knew she wanted to be home before dark, so she continued on with the task she'd been dreading for so long.

Walking to the edge of the overlook, Claire looked out across the sweeping valley below. There were sparse patches of green leaves on some of the trees, a sign that a new season of promises was on the way.

Claire knelt, placed the box on the ground and untied the twine from it. Taking a long, deep breath, she opened the box, revealing the light gray ash inside.

Not wanting to allow her self a second to think about it, she tipped the box over and watched as the fine, light gray ash spilled out and blew gently away.

Watching till the box was empty, tears ran quietly down her cheeks. Her heart ached like never before, and Claire whispered through her tears, "*Forever Daniel. I'll love you forever.*"

Suddenly, the little red bird swooped down near her and then soared out over the valley, it's wings outspread as it glided away from Claire.

Realizing she needed to head back to her house before dark, she knew she needed to turn back soon. As she walked back at a brisk pace, trying to beat the darkness, Claire's dried tears streaked her face.

Although her heart still ached, she knew she'd just taken another step toward healing.

That night, snuggled beneath her cozy quilt of memories, Claire slept deeply, dreaming of Daniel. And of Matt.

Chapter 22

"Here, let me help you!" Claire said, rushing down the back steps to help Matt bring his tools up onto the porch and out of the pouring rain.

"I've got it! Don't get wet!" he said, scooping up his rotating saw and unplugging it quickly.

"This rain has been threatening all day," Claire said, ignoring Matt's comment and hurrying to pick up the orange extension cord from the yard.

"Oh, I was about ready to take a break anyway," Matt said, wiping the raindrops from his hair.

"Here, come in and let me get you a towel," Claire said, holding the back door open for Matt.

As they sat at her kitchen table, Claire sipped hot tea and Matt drank coffee as the driving rain continued outside.

"This is really a soaker!" Matt said, looking over Claire's shoulder and out the window behind her.

"I love it when it rains though," Claire said, "The sound. The smell. I've always loved it, ever since I was young."

"Me, too," Matt said, "There's something so relaxing about it, isn't there?" Taking a sip from his mug, he added, "So, tell me more about your plans."

"Well," Claire began, pleased to have someone to talk to about her plans, "I've really thought a lot about it, and I think you're right. This place has so much to offer. And, if I love it so much, then others will too!"

"Well, if you're going to want me to put on an addition for you, we need to do it now, before I get too much further on the exterior work. It'll mean more work later if we wait."

"You know," Claire began, thoughtfully, "I do. I do want the addition. And we absolutely need another bathroom in the house. We've needed another one for years! So, yes, I think we should go ahead."

Smiling, Matt said nothing, but liked the way Claire used the word 'we' in her plans now.

"What?" she said, smiling now her self, "Why are you grinning at me?"

"Oh, nothing," Matt said, "Just glad to hear you're giving it a go!"

Claire contacted Daniel's old business partner in Florida and had plans drawn-up for the addition. Mr. Wimbley knew the right people in town who could help Claire get the seal of approval for her new bed-and-breakfast business. And, truth be known, the locals were thrilled to have a new business coming to their little mountain town.

Matt had truckloads of building materials hauled up the mountain and delivered immediately. And Matt's sister, Annie, put Claire in touch with the right officials to inspect and license her B&B.

Claire's plans were all falling neatly into place. And she was happier than she'd been in months, content to have a new project and a new purpose.

Several weeks later, Matt and a friend of his had framed-in the new addition, extended the hip roof, installed new plumbing and hung drywall.

"I can't believe all you've gotten done already!" Claire said, surveying the new walls.

"Couldn't have done it without my buddy's help," Matt told her.

"Well, the wood flooring will be here soon!" Claire said, "And I've got some new furniture and linens coming."

"You've really thought this thing out, haven't you?" Matt said, looking down from atop an extension ladder.

"Well, I've still got some details to work out," Claire said, "But it's coming together!"

"I've heard the locals are thrilled to have another place that'll provide lodging for the tourists and keep them in town longer," Matt said.

"Don't forget the county will still want to come out and do the final inspections, when we're ready!" Claire said, brushing the drywall dust from her jeans.

"We'll be ready!" Matt said, again liking the sound of 'we' in Claire's plans.

For weeks, Matt continued working on the addition, installing trims and fixtures, painting, installing lighting and putting the finishing touches on the new bedroom and bathroom.

One afternoon, as Claire was vacuuming the baseboards and cleaning the final construction dust, she looked up to see a man at her door, through the glass storm door. She turned off the vacuum and ran a hand through her tousled hair.

"Hello, ma'am!" the uniformed man said, "Your husband is up on the roof and told me I'd find you inside."

"Oh, he's not my..." Claire began, "Oh, uh, never mind. Sorry."

"Well, I have a furniture delivery for you today, ma'am!"

"Oh!" Claire said, excited to be able to finally set-up her guest rooms. "Yes, I've been expecting you! I'm so glad you're here!"

For the next hour-and-a-half, the deliveryman and his young helper carried furniture pieces in to the house, to the new bedroom, the living room, and finally, up the wooden stairs, under Claire's direction.

"The armoire goes in the corner, please," she directed, as the men carried the last piece into a guest room.

"Did you just buy this place?" the man asked, setting the piece carefully on the hardwood floor.

"Oh, no!" Claire explained, "We've had the house for years. I'm just opening a new bed and breakfast now!"

"Well, I'll be sure to let folks know about this place!" the man said. "It's beautiful out here!"

And with that, he turned to walk out of the bedroom, only to bump into Matt.

"'Scuse me, sir," he said, as he and Matt squeezed passed one another in the tiny alcove entry to the bedroom.

"Sure," Matt said. "Is Claire in…"

"Right here!" Claire called from around the corner.

"Hey," Matt continued, "I'm thinking about running into town for a burger. Want to come?"

"Like this?" Claire asked, laughing, as she looked down at her faded jeans and then put a hand on her hair.

"Ah, come on," Matt urged. "You want folks to know you get your hands dirty out at this fancy place! Builds character!"

"Well, if you don't mind being seen with me like this," Claire joked.

"It'll boost my reputation around these parts to be seen with the most beautiful woman in town! I'm game, if you are!" Matt said, winking at Claire and grinning as he placed a hand on the small of her back to lead her from the room.

Chapter 23

Matt and Claire were sitting in an oversized booth in the small diner in town.

"Here we go!" the waitress said, placing two plates of huge burgers with fries before Matt and Claire.

"Best burger you've ever had!" Matt said as Claire started pouring ketchup on her fries.

"I've never *seen* a cheeseburger this big!" Claire laughed.

"Yeah," Matt said, "I'm glad I can eat these now and then. I missed them!"

"Now and then?" Claire asked, wondering what Matt meant.

"Long story," he said, "I had to lay off this kind of stuff for a while after my surgery."

Again sensing that Matt didn't want to talk about his previous health problems, Claire said, "Mmmm, it's delicious!"

Looking across the table at Claire, Matt smiled, and then used his napkin to wipe the ketchup from the edge of her mouth.

Laughing, Claire said, "Thank you."

"You have the best laugh," Matt said, "I always love to hear you laugh."

Self-conscious, and beginning to blush, Claire said, "Oh! Thank you. It's been a while since I've actually felt like laughing, believe me."

"So, how're you doing, anyway?" Matt asked.

"Better, much better," Claire said sincerely. "I'm really surprised, myself, actually. It's been just over a year, but in the first days after Daniel's death, I thought I'd never get through it."

"I'll bet," Matt said, taking a bite, "But you're a really strong woman, Claire."

"Everyone always tells me that," Claire said, raising her eyebrows, "But, I really didn't feel so strong in the beginning."

Swallowing hard, and wanting to change the subject, she asked, "So what about you? Were you ever married?"

"Almost," Matt said, suddenly looking sad as if he'd just been reminded of something uncomfortable. "But I couldn't do that to someone… Become a burden, I mean."

"A *burden*?" Claire asked, "How?"

"My health was up and down so much and she really wanted to have kids," he explained. "It took all I had to break it off with her, but I did it for *her*."

"That is about the most unselfish thing I've ever heard," Claire said, seeing Matt in a new light and also seeing the hurt still in his eyes.

"So," she went on, "Is your health better now?"

"Yep! Good as new!" he answered, smiling again, as the waitress placed their check on the table.

"Any dessert today, Matt?" the waitress asked.

"Claire? For you?" Matt said, looking across the table.

"Oh, no!" she said. "I don't know where I'd put it!"

"Oh, Hey, Gail," Matt said to the waitress, "By the way, this is Claire Mitchell. She's opening that new B&B down the road."

"I heard about your place!" the waitress said, obviously surprising Claire that she knew about the B&B.

"This is a small town! Believe me, Hon!" the waitress went on, seeing Claire's surprise. "Everybody knows *everything* 'round here! Believe me!"

Driving back to her house after lunch, Claire told Matt that she'd received the final licensing papers for the business and had passed the county inspections of the property.

"So how are you advertising for your guests?" Matt asked.

"I've put ads in travel magazines and Elaine has advertised it on the Internet for me, listing my phone number up here as

183

a contact," Claire explained. "But that was just recently, after I got the go-ahead from the county, so I haven't had any responses yet."

"Once people see your place," Matt said, "I'll bet you have regulars every year."

"I hope so!" Claire said, climbing down from Matt's big, red truck after he'd parked behind her house.

"No, really! I mean it!" Matt went on, looking around outside Claire's house. "Look at what you've done out here!"

It was true. Claire had made her vision a reality for the old home. The sideboards were now a freshly painted pale yellow and she'd selected a warm, creamy salmon color for the trim, shutters and doors on the house.

She'd had Matt paint the wood floors on the front and back porches with a soft, muted light gray color. Then, Claire had hung huge welcoming wreaths on the exterior doors.

She'd bought four more rocking chairs and had Matt paint the old ones with a new coat of white paint. Inspired by the gazebo she'd seen at the Willows B&B, Claire put a large, white gazebo beside the pond and had put bench seating in it. Vines were intertwined in the lattice on the gazebo and tiny pink flowers were just beginning to bloom.

Several picnic tables sat at the pond's edge, so guests could sit outside and enjoy the glorious mountainous scenery. And Claire had put Daniel's little aluminum boat at the water's edge, where it sat waiting for Claire's first guests.

"Yeah," Claire said, smiling and looking around at the home's transformation, "I'm pretty happy with it. And I really appreciate all the work you've done out here, Matt!"

"This was my favorite project that I've ever done," Matt said. "Honestly, I'll miss coming out here every day."

Claire realized she'd miss having Matt at her house every day too. "Believe me," she said, "The upkeep on this place will keep us busy! I'm sure I'll still need some help!"

"Now *that's* what I like to hear!" Matt said, grinning, and buoyed at the hope of keeping Claire in his life.

For the next few weeks, Claire busied herself around her house, enjoying handling all the details of her exciting new venture. She'd sewn window toppers and drapes for all the windows, mixing coordinating plaid and floral fabrics in shades of light peach, creamy yellow and soft blue colors.

She'd made over-stuffed throw pillows and had even sewn coordinating dresser scarves with the fabric remnants. She lovingly polished the older furniture in the house that she'd decided to keep and she placed her new area rugs atop the hardwood floors with Matt's help. Deciding to keep Daniel's mother's treasured hand-hooked wool rug in the living room, she'd had it professionally cleaned.

A new, sunny yellow jacquard tablecloth atop the long farmhouse table in her kitchen and yellow, plaid window toppers above the kitchen windows gave her kitchen a cozy, fresh, welcoming feel.

The house was an eclectic mix of old and new, tastefully brought together with Claire's own expertise. Surveying the house's new look, Claire realized that just like the old house, she, too, was also a revised version of her former self, a mix of both old and new, with years of memories and stories hidden behind the exterior.

Chapter 24

Just as Claire was removing a tin of hot muffins from her oven, Matt drove into the yard with a truckload of plants that Claire had asked him to pick-up in town for her.

"Well, hey, there, pretty lady!" he said, stepping into the kitchen, used to coming in to the house now without knocking.

"Just in time!" Claire said, turning the muffins onto a cooling rack.

"Mmmm! Smells good in here!" Matt said, hanging his lightweight jacket on the wall hook near the door, just as if he'd done it a thousand times before.

"Well, I'm afraid that you're my guinea pig!" Claire told him. "This is a new recipe!"

"Always happy to be of service, you know!" Matt said, reaching for a hot muffin.

"Careful," Claire warned, as Matt broke open the fresh-baked muffin, allowing steam to rise from it, and then taking a bite.

"Mmmm!" he said appreciatively, chewing the muffin, "What's in here?"

"Secret recipe," Claire joked.

"Then I'll just have to come *here* to get my muffins, I guess," Matt said.

"You'll get no arguments from me on *that* one!"

Absentmindedly, standing next to Claire, Matt reached over and rubbed her back a couple times,

"You're a woman of many talents, Claire Mitchell!"

Claire realized she was pleased and slightly warmed by Matt's touch and actually comfortable with his hand on her.

"Well, I just hope our guests are as easy to please as you are!" she joked.

'That word again,' Matt thought, '*Our*.' He loved the sound of it.

"Oh!" Claire remembered. "Guess *what*? I have my first two reservations!"

"Congrats!" Matt said. "You are officially in the bed and breakfast business, ma'am!"

"Yeah!" Claire said excitedly. "I was thrilled to get the calls! One is an older couple who've been coming up this way for years and the other couple is coming here to celebrate their first wedding anniversary."

"They're gonna just love this place, Claire. You've done wonders with it! Really!" Matt said.

A couple weeks before Claire's first guests were to arrive, Layne and Danny drove up from Florida for a visit.

"Mom!" Layne said, stepping from car, almost before Danny had even stopped it.

Claire was running down the back steps, grinning, arms outstretched and with tears in her eyes.

"Oh! I've missed you two SO much!" she said, hugging Layne tightly, then turning next to Danny who'd walked up to the two tearful women as they embraced.

"Danny! I'm so glad to see you guys!" Claire said excitedly.

"Wow!" Danny said, looking past his mom at the house. "The place looks amazing!"

"I can't believe it's the even same house!" Layne said, amazed at the transformation and looking around at the gazebo and the picnic tables beside the lake.

"Well, come inside," Claire said eagerly, "I can't wait to show you everything we've done!"

Danny couldn't help but catch the word 'we' that his mom had used, but he didn't ask for details.

Walking into the kitchen from the back door, Layne exclaimed, "Oh my gosh! Look at the cabinets! And the windows! And this floor!"

"It's been quite the undertaking!" Claire said.

"I couldn't believe it when we heard you're making it into a B&B," Danny said.

"Layne and I thought you'd finally lost your mind, honestly!"

"Yeah, but now..." Layne trailed off, stepping into the living room. "Now that I see it all, I really get it!"

"Oh, Mom!" she said excitedly, seeing Daniel's photo on the mantle over the brick fireplace. "I love this one of Daddy!"

"Me, too," Claire said, smiling. "I had it in my bedroom, but I want our guests to know your dad too, so I put it out here. After all, it was *his* family's house, long before I ever came into the picture."

"Dad would be just blown away by this place!" Danny said, looking at the new drapes that hung from ceiling to floor framing each new living room window.

"And we were worried that you were bored up here!" Layne said. "You haven't had *time* to be bored, have you?"

Claire showed Layne and Danny the upstairs bedrooms, complete with new furnishings, bedding and window coverings.

"I'm so glad you kept the some of the original wood floors," Layne said.

"They're part of the charm, I think," Claire said as Layne and Danny followed her downstairs again. "Now, come and have a look at the new bedroom addition and the new bathrooms I had put in."

"I thought you were only adding one new bathroom, Mom," Danny said. "Yeah, but when Matt and I talked, he suggested that I needed my own, private bathroom, entirely separate from the guests," Claire explained.

"Hmmm, I think I need to meet this *Matt guy*, Mom," Danny said protectively. "Sounds like he's around here an awful lot."

"He *was* my contractor, Danny," Claire said defensively. "And he's a nice guy! You'll like him!"

"This is incredible!" Layne exclaimed, looking at the bathroom right off of Claire's own bedroom. "Where'd you find this beautiful old claw foot tub?" she asked.

"Oh, it's not really an antique," Claire explained. "I found it through one of my distributors."

"Could've fooled *me*! It's looks vintage!" Layne said, next admiring the white wainscoting on the lower walls of the bathroom.

"I was going to put it in the new bathroom for the guests, but at the last minute, I decided I just had to keep it for myself!" Claire explained.

Walking through the living room and into the newly added guest bedroom, Danny admired the wood flooring in the addition.

"Yeah," Claire said, "I wanted to match it as best I could with the old floors. Give it some continuity, you know."

"*Look* at this bed!" Layne said, running her hand down a poster of the four-poster bed. "What a romantic room, Mom!"

"I like it," Claire said. "And there's a door on the back of this room that leads to the backside of the little bathroom, so the guests will have some privacy."

"This Matt-guy does nice work," Danny said approvingly, as he surveyed the crown molding at the ceiling. "Dad would approve of this craftsmanship."

"Well, I hope you two will approve of Matt," Claire said, "Because I've invited him for dinner."

"Ah, you've invited your '*contractor*' for dinner?" Danny said with an air of skepticism.

"He's heard all about you and Layne," Claire said, "And I want him to meet you. I'm proud of you two!"

"We'd like to meet him, Mom," Layne said, turning around and rolling her eyes at her older and overly-protective brother, "Wouldn't *we*, Danny?"

Chapter 25

As the sun was just beginning to set behind the mountains, Matt's red truck pulled into the yard.

"You're obviously overpaying him, Mom," Danny said, looking out the kitchen window at Matt's new truck.

"What?" Claire said, removing a roast from the oven.

"That's an awfully nice truck for a country contractor," Danny said. "So, either you're overpaying him or he really doesn't need the work if he's driving *that*!"

"Danny!" Claire said, clearly becoming exasperated with her son.

Shaking hands firmly with Matt, Danny said, "Nice to meet you, Matt. Mom hasn't told us very much about you."

Trying to cover her brother's rudeness, Layne extended her hand to Matt. "Ah, what my brother means, is that my mom hasn't *had* to tell us much about you. Your work speaks for itself! The place looks beautiful!"

Relieved that Layne was more receptive to his presence, Matt said, "Well, your mom has told me *all* about both of you! She was really excited that you were coming for a few days!"

Looking past Layne, Matt said, "Hi, Claire!" smiling and presenting her a bouquet of cut flowers. "These are for the best cook in town!"

"So, you've eaten here *before*, then?!" Danny interjected, shocked that Matt had obviously been at the house more than he'd at first known.

"Um, well… once or twice ~ sure," Claire said uncomfortably. "While he was working on the house, you know."

"Uh-huh. I see," Danny mumbled, stepping onto the back porch for some air.

Layne followed her brother outside. "Excuse me just a minute," she said to Matt as she closed the door behind her so could speak to her brother privately.

"You've got two great kids," Matt said to Claire.

"Well, I have to apologize for Danny's attitude," Claire said, shocked her self at Danny's rudeness.

"No need for any apology!" Matt laughed. "I respect a man who looks after the women in his life. Really. You're a special person, Claire. I don't blame him one bit for being skeptical of a strange man in his mom's house."

"Well, thank you," Claire said, feeling relieved and looking into Matt's eyes appreciatively.

"What is *your* problem?" Layne asked Danny, as he rocked furiously in a rocker on the back porch.

Danny didn't answer, but kept looking out over the pond and rocking.

"He's here for dinner! He's hungry! Big deal!" Layne said irritated with her brother.

"Yeah!" Danny said, smirking. "He's *hungry* all right! I can clearly see that he's got an appetite for *some*thing!"

"Lower your voice!" Layne told her brother in a whisper.

"Layne, are you blind, or *what*?!" Danny said, looking furiously at his sister. "He's got it bad for Mom!"

"Danny, come on," Layne said, sitting in the rocker beside Danny and placing her hand on his arm. "Dad's been gone for more than a year now. *He* would want Mom to be happy. Don't *you*?"

"Of course I do!" Danny said. "But I can't even think about Mom with anyone else but DAD!"

"Mom is alone now, Danny," Layne explained. "Dad wouldn't want her to be alone. Trust me. And neither do I."

Shaking his head, Danny took a deep breath. "I know. I know. But Mom is completely oblivious to this guy's intentions!"

"Uh, Mom is a lot smarter than you think, Danny," Layne said. "She's given me some of the best advice I've had in my lifetime. She can take care of herself. Believe me."

"Dad would want me to look after her!" Danny said.

"Okay," Layne answered. "Then, give this guy a chance. You don't even know him yet!"

Realizing that his sister was right, Danny stopped rocking. "Okay. A *chance*. I can do that," he said, standing up.

"Smells good, Mom!" Danny said, stepping back inside the kitchen.

"We're almost ready," Claire said, silently hoping that Danny would be more pleasant during dinner.

The dinner conversation was easy and pleasant. "This is great!" Matt said, referring to Claire's roast.

"Thanks," she said. "My mom's recipe, actually."

"Has MeMa seen this place, Mom? I mean since you did all this," Layne asked.

"No, not yet," Claire said. "She's traveling right now, actually. Big surprise, right?"

"What about Aunt El?" Danny asked.

"She saw it in the very early stages," Claire explained. "But I've sent her pictures."

"I've talked to her," Layne said. "She thinks you're crazy for doing the B&B at all! She keeps in touch with me at school."

"I know," Claire laughed. "And maybe I am. But, I'll never know if I don't give it a try!"

"Oh, listen, Danny," Matt said, serving himself more mashed potatoes, "I was hoping you'd help me move some of those big beams from behind the house while you're here. I could use a hand lifting them, if you don't mind."

"Sure," Danny said, purposely not making eye contact with Matt.

After dinner, while Layne and Claire washed the dishes, Matt and Danny went outside.

"Here," Matt said, pointing to four long ten-inch square beams, "Can you just grab an end?"

"Got it," Danny said, picking up an end.

After they'd carried the second beam to the storage shed, Matt said, "Danny, listen. I think we got off on the wrong foot."

Danny listened, not saying a word, and Matt went on. "Your mom and I are just friends. Nothing more. I don't want you to get the wrong idea."

"You always bring flowers for your *friends*, huh?" Danny said.

"Hmmm. Good point," Matt said, as the two stopped walking and looked at one another. "Listen, man to man. As I said, your mom and I are just friends. But, yes, she's a beautiful woman. That's no secret to anyone. And, in different circumstances, maybe things could be different, but I really respect your mother, Danny."

Taking a deep breath, "So, I was right. You *would* like to be more than friends with Mom."

"If your mom only has room in her life right now for a *friend*," Matt explained, "I can be just a friend. If *she* ever wants any *more* than that, then it'll be *her* call. I hope you can respect that."

"I just want what's best for Mom," Danny said. "It hit her so hard when we lost Dad."

"I know," Matt said. "*Anyone* can tell that your mom loved – no, that she *loves* – your dad. He was one lucky guy."

"Hey, guys!" Claire called from the kitchen window, "Anyone for molten chocolate lava cake?"

"Be *right* there!" Matt called. Then, looking at Danny, he continued. "I want what's best for your mom too. Whatever *she* wants."

Relenting slightly, Danny said, "Okay. I believe you. Sorry about the attitude before dinner."

Matt smiled and extended his hand to Danny. "Your mom's lucky to have a son like you, Danny. Really. I mean it. Says a lot about the man that your dad was too!"

Chapter 26

For the next three days, Claire spent all her time with Layne and Danny. The trio was nearly inseparable, eating together by the lake, hiking through the woods and alongside the stream on the property, just like they had done countless times before, year after year.

"Mom," Layne asked one afternoon, as they all walked along a path near the house, "What about Dad's ashes?"

"I took them up to the look-out," Claire said.

"Good," Layne said. "That's perfect."

"Dad always loved it up here," Danny said. "And I'm really glad you held on to the house."

"I'll always keep it for you kids," Claire said, "Like we'd always planned."

"Sounds like we may need to make a reservation to stay at the house next time though!" Danny joked. "

Be careful, guys!" she answered, "Or I just might put you to work cooking or cleaning for our guests!"

The next morning, Claire stood outside, hugging Layne and Danny as they prepared to drive back to Florida.

"And, Mom," Danny said, "You watch that new guy!"

"Matt?" Claire said, laughing. "No worries there!"

As Layne hugged her mom tightly, she whispered, "Ignore Danny, Mom! Matt's a great guy! Not to mention the fact that he's not too hard on the eyes either!"

Smiling, Claire released Layne, with tears forming again in her eyes.

"You two be careful now! Watch that lead foot, Danny! I love you both!"

And Claire watched as Danny's car disappeared down the dirt road and out of sight.

Later that afternoon, Mr. Wimbley stopped by for a visit. "Hiya, Claire!" he said, closing the door of his old pick-up.

Claire stood up from where she was planting her new bedding plants, brushing herself off.

"Mr. Wimbley! What a nice surprise!"

"Came by to have a look at the place," he said, looking at the house. "Matt told me all you've done out here and I wanted to have a look for myself!"

"Oh, yes, I've been meaning to thank you for referring Matt to me," Claire said. "He's been a tremendous help to me!"

"Well, he thinks highly of you, too, Claire," Mr. Wimbley said, casting a sideward, knowing glance toward Claire. "The missus and I think he's smitten!"

"Oh, no," Claire protested, shaking her head. "We're just friends."

"Call it what you want, Claire, but we've never seen that boy like this! He lights up like a Christmas tree at the mention of your name! You just might be the best medicine that boy's had yet!"

Feeling a bit uncomfortable, Claire tried to change the subject. "Well, let me show you around," she said, gesturing toward the back steps. "Come on in!"

Half an hour later, Mr. Wimbley and Claire were outside once again. "The place is beautiful!" he said, "I can't believe all you've done out here! What have you named your B&B?"

"Oh my gosh!" Claire said. "Would you believe I haven't thought of that? I've done all the licensing in my name, as the proprietor, but I guess I need to consider that, don't I?"

"Well, get a feel for the new place first!" Mr. Wimbley said. "It'll come to you! A name will come to you and you'll know it's right!"

The night before her first guests were to arrive, Claire was polishing the antique door handle on the new front door when Matt drove up.

"You can stop now!" he joked, stepping from his truck. "I think they can eat off your floors!"

"Nervous energy!" Claire said, laughing. "What brings you out here?"

Reaching into the bed of his truck, Matt pulled out two fishing rods and a tackle box. "Thought you might want these for your guests!"

"Oh!" Claire said, "Well there are a couple rods in the basement, but…"

"Yeah, but you'll want Danny to have his dad's fishing rods one day," Matt said. "Just let people use these instead and keep Dan's for Danny one day."

"I hadn't even considered that!" Claire said, touched by Matt's thoughtfulness, especially considering Danny's skeptical attitude toward him.

"No problem!" Matt grinned. "Plus, it was a good excuse for me to see you again today!"

Laughing, Claire said, "Well, thank you! This was so kind of you! Do you want to come inside?"

"Nah," Matt said, "It's your last free evening for a few days! Enjoy it! I'll check in on you though!"

The next morning, as Claire was hanging new white bathrobes in the bathroom for the guests, she heard a car pull up outside. Going outside to greet her first guests, she said, "You must be the McKinneys! Welcome!"

"Your directions were perfect!" the older man said, "But, did I miss the sign by the road?"

"Oh, no," Claire replied, "I haven't put one up yet."

"Well, your place is even more beautiful than the ad described!" he said, carrying two suitcases, "Let's keep it our secret then, shall we?"

Chapter 27

Claire spent the new two days enjoying the slow and easy pace of having just one couple as guests in her house. She prepared full breakfasts for the McKinneys each morning. She treated them to hot tea with scones and fresh cream or her homemade lemon pound cake and espresso in the late afternoons.

"Claire," Mrs. McKinney said, holding her teacup, "You're an incredible host! We certainly never expected all this!"

"I've always wanted to own a bed and breakfast," Claire explained, "I think I'm really going to like it!"

On the third day of her new venture, Claire's next guests arrived. The Paulsons were a young couple from Seattle and were celebrating their first wedding anniversary.

Claire envied both of the couples in her home. She noticed how the McKinneys, married for over forty years, still held hands as they walked around the pond. And also how the Paulsons loved to excitedly talk about their plans for the future and their eagerness to have children. Claire realized that she and Daniel fell 'somewhere in the middle' of the two couples. They had *been* the young couple in love with their whole future ahead of them. And yet their plans had been cut short before they could be like the McKinneys, chatting about their retirement, and sharing photos of their beloved grandchildren.

Daydreaming one morning, as she waited for the timer to signal that her baked muffins were ready, Claire was shaken back into reality by Mr. McKinney's voice from the bathroom.

"Claire!" he said, his voice coming closer, as he hurried to the kitchen in his white bathrobe. "The water! I think a pipe burst in the wall at the tub!"

"Oh, no!" Claire said, running into the bathroom to find water everywhere. "Excuse me!" she said, rushing from of the bathroom and past the Paulsons who were in the doorway trying to see what all the commotion was about.

Claire hurried to the basement to turn off the water supply to the house. Rushing down the steep wooden steps, though, she missed a step and tumbled down the last few steps, landing on the hard, cold cement floor below.

Trying to stand, Claire winced as she tried to put weight on her right foot. Looking down, she saw her ankle was already swelling.

Still intent on stopping the deluge upstairs, Claire leaned on a vertical beam for support, then against the washer, as she made her way, in little 'hops,' to the newly installed shut-off valve under the stairs. Pain was searing through her ankle and her foot was swelling quickly, but her adrenaline gave Claire the strength she needed to get to the valve. Reaching to turn the handle, Claire saw the old carving on the backside of the wooden steps again.

"Daniel," she said, tears filling her eyes, she turned off the water and then slumped against the washer.

"Claire?" Robert Paulson called from the top of the stairs. "You okay down there?"

"Uh, I'm not so sure at the moment," Claire called out, hearing Robert hurrying down the steps toward her.

"Oh! Your head!" he said, as soon as he saw Claire. Reaching up, Claire felt the wet blood on her forehead. Looking at the blood in her hand, she said, "I didn't even realize I'd hit my head! It's my ankle that's killing me!"

"Let me call someone!" Robert said. "An ambulance or something!"

"You're from the city, for sure!" Claire said. "I don't even think they *have* ambulances up here in the mountains!"

"Well, then, let me get you to a doctor!" he said, helping Claire to lean her weight on him and slightly lifting her with his arm around her waist.

Claire made her way slowly up the steps, leaning on Robert for support, careful not to put weight on her injured ankle.

Limping into the kitchen, Claire was met by the McKinneys and Robert's wife, Amanda, all standing in their bathrobes, looking wide-eyed, first at Claire's bleeding head and then at her swollen, purple ankle.

"Here!" Mr. McKinney said, pulling out a kitchen chair. "You, sit down! Let me get some ice!"

"I've got it!" Mrs. McKinney said, rushing to the freezer and placing ice cubes in a nearby dishtowel.

"Here you go, Honey," she said, handing Claire the ice pack. "Hold this on your ankle. I'll get something for your head."

"I'm calling 9-1-1!" Amanda said, reaching for the phone hanging on the wall.

"I don't think we even *have* a 9-1-1 system up here," Claire said, wincing as she propped her foot on another chair.

"You're right," Amanda said, looking quizzically at the phone receiver in her hand.

"Hey," she said, looking at the corkboard by the phone, "Who's this Mr.

Wimbley whose number is here? A neighbor or a friend?"

"Yeah," Claire said, "Could you call him and ask if he knows who the nearest doctor might be?"

As Amanda was dialing the phone, the timer on the oven went off, only adding to the chaotic scene.

"Oh!" Claire said, trying to stand up, "My muffins!"

"Sit down, Hon!" Mrs. McKinney said. "I know my way around a kitchen after four children and seven grandchildren! Believe me!"

"Oh, thank you," Claire said, feeling weary and embarrassed. "I'm so sorry about all of this!" she said, sighing.

"Nonsense!" Mr. McKinney said, placing a hand on Claire's shoulder. "We don't mind a bit. These things happen."

"Mr. Wimbley said he'd call the doctor and have him come right over," Amanda said, hanging up the phone.

"Come OVER?" Claire said. "We're not in Kansas anymore, are we? These mountain doctors really do still make house calls, I guess!"

"Sounds like you haven't lived here that long, yourself!" Mr. McKinney said to Claire.

"It's a long story!" Claire said. "We've… *I've* owned the house for a while, but I lived in Florida till I decided to come up here after…." But, Claire stopped

209

herself. Moments later, she began to explain that the house had belonged to her husband's parents and she'd decided to keep it after Daniel had died.

"That can't be the doctor *already*!" Amanda said, looking out the kitchen window into the back yard. "It's two men in a red truck."

Suddenly the door to the kitchen burst open.

"Claire! My God!" Matt said, seeing Claire holding ice to her head with her bruised and swollen ankle propped on a chair.

"Matt!" Claire said, shocked to see both Matt and Mr. Wimbley. "How'd *you* know?"

"Never mind," he said, moving the dishtowel from Claire's head. "Let me see that!"

"Doctor Ward's on the way over," Mr. Wimbley said, looking at Claire's head. "That's a nasty bump on your noggin, Hon!"

"It's actually my ankle that's killing me though," Claire said, looking at her disfigured purple ankle propped on a kitchen chair.

"We need to get you to a hospital," Matt said. "The closest one is nearly an hour away though."

"No!" Claire protested. "Let's just wait for the doctor. My head probably looks worse than it really IS! I've got two kids. I've dealt with this kinda stuff before! Trust me!"

"Ah! Here's Doc Ward now!" Mr. Wimbley said, opening the door for Doctor Ward, who came in carrying a black satchel, like Claire had imagined he'd done for the last fifty years.

"You must be Claire Mitchell!" Doctor ward said, putting his satchel on the kitchen table. "I've heard all about you in town!"

"Did you hear that I'm clumsy too?" Claire joked.

"I haven't been inside this house for years," Doctor Ward said. "It's one of my favorite houses 'round here! Used to go fishin' out back with Dan years back!"

"With my husband?" Claire asked.

"Oh, Heavens no!" Doc Ward answered. "With your husband's father, Dan *Senior*!"

"You've been around here for a WHILE then, haven't you?" Claire asked, realizing that Doctor Ward must be over eighty years old.

"MmmHmm," Doc Ward answered, touching Claire's head.

"Ouch!" she winced, pulling away slightly.

"Well, I don't think you'll need any stitches," he said, next pointing an offending light in Claire's eyes to check the dilation of her pupils and causing her to blink rapidly.

"Looks good," he said, to no one in particular. "Let's see that ankle now," he said, gently moving Claire's foot.

"MmmHmm. MmmHmm," he murmured. "Not broken," he said. "Sprained pretty good though, I'd say."

"I want to take her to the hospital in Roanoke," Matt said. "I think we should get an x-ray."

"Well, you certainly could do that, Matt," Doc Ward said. "But I've dealt with these things, a time or two, you know."

"Sorry, Doc," Matt said, not wanting to offend the kindly old doctor. "You were really good to me when I needed you. I'm sure you know what you're doing! I'm just worried about her, that's all."

"You know, if I can bandage this head up, and get some aspirin, I'll be okay, I think," Claire said.

"I can fix you right up!" Doc Ward said, pulling a roll of bandage material from his bag. "We'll need to keep a close eye on you though, Claire," he said, "I don't want you to go to sleep for a while, but I DO want you to stay off of this foot."

"I just need some crutches…" Claire began.

"No, ma'am! I said stay OFF of that foot!" Doc Ward said, more forcefully this time.

"But I've got guests," Claire said, looking around at the McKinneys and the Paulsons in their bathrobes.

"And I've got a flooded bathroom! And now I can't turn on the water till that's fixed! And I need to get another batch of muffins in the oven! And… and… " she said, tears welling up in her eyes.

"Relax," Matt said calmly, placing a hand on Claire's shoulder, "It's no problem."

"But I…" Claire began.

"We'll work it out, Claire," he said calmly, suddenly realizing that it was he who was using the word 'we' now.

Suddenly, Claire felt reassured, even protected, for the first time in a long time.

As Doctor Ward left, he offered Mr. Wimbley a ride. "That'd be great," Mr. Wimbley answered, winking at Matt over Claire's shoulder, "Looks like Matt may be busy around here for a bit!"

"I'll just have a look at the plumbing," Matt said, "And get things cleaned up over here."

"Oh, Matt," Claire said gratefully, "I can't thank you enough for all your help."

"Happy to help!" Matt said. "I doubt you'll be polishing doorknobs or baking muffins for a while from the looks of it!"

Hours later, Mrs. McKinney and Amanda had finished baking the muffins, using the rest of Claire's prepared batter. They'd tidied up Claire's kitche, done all the laundry and tended to Claire while Matt worked on the plumbing repairs.

Mr. McKinney and Robert had gone into town to pick-up the plumbing parts Matt had requested.

"And now for the moment of truth!" Matt said, heading down to the basement to turn on the main water valve.

"I think you've fixed it, Matt!" Robert called from the bathroom moments later.

"Thank goodness!" Claire said, relieved that Matt was able to repair the plumbing so her guests wouldn't be even further inconvenienced.

"Like Doc Ward said," Matt joked, coming into the living room, "I've done this a time or two!"

Claire laughed at Matt's impersonation of Doc Ward, obviously relieved that order was being restored to her house.

"It's good to see you laugh, Claire," Matt said, "You've got such a great laugh."

Smiling, Claire said, "It *feels* good to laugh again. Thanks."

"Here we are!" Mrs. McKinney said in her sing-song voice, "Some hot tea for you, my dear!"

"You've *really* got to stop waiting on me like this! You're MY guests!" Claire insisted. "I'm really so embarrassed by all this!"

"Nonsense," Mrs. McKinney said, handing Claire a cup and saucer with steaming herbal tea. "I'm just glad we were *here* when you took that nasty tumble! You just need to rest now!"

"Honestly, I've never seen Claire sit still for so long!" Matt joked.

"Well, I've got to be up and around!" Claire said defiantly. "I've got guests!"

"No, ma'am!" Matt said. "I've got that covered. You're staying off that foot like Doc Ward told you!"

"What? But how?" Claire asked, confused by Matt's comment.

Chapter 28

The next morning, Claire awoke to the smell of bacon and warm bread before her alarm had even beeped. Touching her forehead, she instantly remembered the fall she'd taken the day before, and she also realized that her ankle was throbbing again.

Sitting up slowly, she could see Matt's red truck through the lacy sheers on her window. She lay back down, smiling, and inhaling deeply the comforting smells coming from her kitchen.

"Knock, knock!" Matt said, cracking the bedroom door, "Are you decent, Claire?"

"Uh, yes," she answered, pulling the quilt a bit tighter around her.

"So, how's our patient this morning?" Matt asked, carrying a tray of breakfast for Claire.

"What's all *this*?" Claire asked, grinning.

"Just a little nourishment and a couple of aspirin, which I figured you'd need again," he said, placing the tray beside Claire on her bed.

"Oh, my gosh! Breakfast! My guests!" Claire said, sitting upright too quickly, then grabbing her head and wincing.

"Oh, no you don't," Matt said, helping her to lie back again and propping a second pillow behind her for support. "Your guests are having their breakfast out at the pond," he went on, smiling. "I *can* cook, you know! I've been a bachelor for all of my adult life and I do like to eat on occasion!"

"*You*? *You've* already prepared breakfast for *everyone*?" Claire asked, touched by Matt's kind gesture. "But, I didn't even hear them get up!"

"They all wanted to let you sleep," Matt said, handing Claire a mug filled with freshly brewed coffee, "Here you go."

Claire carefully took a sip at Matt's insistence, and then she swallowed the aspirin he'd handed to her.

I'm not used to all this!" she said, smiling "Thank you so much! *Really*, Matt, I *mean* it. You've been so good to me!"

"Mind if I keep you company while you eat?" Matt asked.

"Of course," Claire said. "I must look frightful though, if I *look* even *half* as awful as I feel!"

"You are just as beautiful as always. Really. I mean it," Matt said, looking earnestly at Claire, and then swallowing hard and clearing his throat.

He pulled a chair closer to the bed as Claire ate her breakfast, feeling a bit self-conscious. "I could get used to this!" she joked.

Fighting the urge to agree with Claire's comment, and tell her that he could get used to seeing her every morning, too, Matt simply said, "My pleasure!"

As Claire finished her breakfast, Matt said, "Oh! I almost forgot! I brought you something! Be right back!"

Moments later, he came back into the room, carrying two metal crutches. "My sister sent these over for you. She had knee surgery a couple years ago, and these have been in her attic. I knew you'd be too stubborn to stay off that ankle for long!"

"Wow! I was just wondering how I'd be getting around for the next few days," Claire said, amazed at Matt's sister's generosity and kindness. "I'm going to have to meet your sister and thank her! First, the fresh donuts…. And now *THIS*! You've both been so kind to me!"

"You deserve it," Matt said. "You've been dealing with a lot lately. And, I am thoroughly enjoying myself, I might add!"

With that, Matt gave her a quick wink and a smile, and took her tray with the empty dishes away. "Let me know if you need help getting up!" he called over his shoulder as he walked out of the bedroom.

"I think I've got it!" Claire said reaching for the crutches Matt had leaned against the wall beside her bed.

An hour later, Claire hobbled into her kitchen on her newfound crutches. Matt's back was to her as he stirred a huge pot on the stove.

"Hey, there!" he said, turning and seeing Claire in the doorway.

"What are you cooking *now*?" Claire asked, shocked to see Matt still working in her kitchen.

"I saw on your bulletin board here that you'd made a note to cook the chicken for chicken salad croissants at 4pm," Matt answered, sprinkling salt in the bubbling pot.

"I was just coming to start that, actually," Claire said, raising her eyebrows in disbelief that Matt had taken charge for her. "Took me a while to get myself together this morning," she added.

"Here you go," Matt said, pulling out a chair for Claire. "You're not putting weight on that ankle just yet today. Here, sit down."

"Matt, really, I …. " Claire protested, "I can do it!"

"I know you CAN," Matt said, smiling, "But, you don't *have* to! I'm at your disposal for as long as you need!"

Laughing, Claire asked, "So, you'll wear the apron too?"

"Oh, no!" he said, laughing. "I can cook, but I draw the line at wearing your apron!"

"I can't *believe* you're doing all this for me," Claire said. "This is not how I'd imagined my first week in business, believe me!"

Well, I understand, from the McKinneys, that they're leaving tomorrow and Robert and Amanda are here for two more days. You're in no shape to be cooking and cleaning and you surely can't handle the stairs, so just sit back and relax."

"Oh, Matt," Claire said, "I really don't know what I'd do without you."

His back to Claire, Matt closed his eyes briefly, soaking in her comment, wishing it meant more than he actually felt that it did.

■■■

Claire leaned on her crutches, watching the McKinneys put their suitcases in their car the next morning. "I'm so sorry for all the chaos," Claire said to Mrs. McKinney.

"We've just enjoyed ourselves so much!" Mrs. McKinney said, hugging Claire. "Don't you worry about a *thing*!"

"We'd like to come back next year," Mr. McKinney added. "If that's okay!"

"I'll look forward to it!" Claire said, buoyed by the McKinney's comments.

"Same time next year?" Matt asked.

"Perfect!" Mr. McKinney replied.

"We'll pencil you in then!" Matt said. "And we should have Internet before long, so we'll e-mail you a confirmation!"

Noticing Matt's usage of the word 'we,' Claire felt comforted and not so alone in her new venture, although she didn't make a comment.

Holding the kitchen door open for Claire, Matt said, "Well, Amanda and Robert headed out to the winery for a bit. Looks like it's just the two of us!"

"You must be exhausted by now!" Claire said. "You were here till late last night, then back again today before dawn! I can handle things around here now. I know you have other things to do besides wait on me!"

"There is *nothing* I'd rather be doing," Matt said, grinning. "I promise! Now, you need to get off that foot!"

Claire spent the morning reading with her foot propped on the sofa. Matt changed the sheets from the Paulsons guest bed, washed and folded all the laundry, tidied the guest room and washed the breakfast dishes, all before noon.

Looking up from her book, Claire found Matt leaning against the doorframe, watching her and smiling, his arms crossed against his chest.

"Oh! I didn't see you there!" she said, closing her book.

"Feel like some lunch yet?" Matt asked.

"I can get myself something!" Claire insisted, "You're making me nervous, waiting on me like this, Matt! Come and sit down a minute, will you?"

An hour later, Claire sat with a green afghan over her lap, and she and Matt chatted comfortably. "So, do you think you'll stay up here year-round then?" Matt asked hopefully.

"I'm really not sure yet," Claire said. "I don't know if I'll like the winters up here as much as being in Florida."

"What would you do back in Florida? Decorating?" Matt asked.

"You'll think I've gone crazy, but I've been doing a lot of thinking. Do you remember how I said I'd always wanted to turn my *Florida* home into a B&B?"

"Uh, yes?" Matt answered hesitantly, not sure he wanted to hear what Claire was about to say.

"Well, I'm thinking about doing it!" Claire said.

"So, you'd close **this** place *already*?" Matt asked, obviously confused, "You haven't even given it a name yet!"

"No! No!" Claire said, shaking her head. "This is the perfect place in the spring and the fall. And the Snowbirds visit Florida in the *winter* months. So, I thought I'd split my time between both places, and keep each B&B open during the appropriate tourist season!"

Deflated at the thought that Claire might be going back to Florida, Matt forced himself to sound happy for her. "Yeah, that might work," he said slowly.

Claire noticed the look on Matt's face, although he'd tried to hide his disappointment. "Ever been to Florida?"

"As a kid a couple times," Matt said. "With my family for vacation. But that's it."

For the next few days, Matt came by to help Claire as her ankle mended, seeing the Paulsons off, then even cleaning their room after they'd gone.

"Well, I think you're in good shape!" he announced one day. "Why don't you call me if you need anything? I'm gonna get going. Got a carpentry job starting soon."

"Matt," Claire said, cautiously, "You've been quiet for the last few days."

"Just been thinking," he answered, looking serious.

"Well," Claire went on, "I hope you know how much I appreciate all you've done for me. I couldn't have gotten through all this without you and I'm grateful."

"Honestly, Claire, I've really enjoyed the last few days and I'm glad you're getting around better," Matt said, forcing a smile.

Chapter 29

Hanging up the phone after speaking with an ad rep at a travel magazine, Claire was excited that she'd just placed her first 'official' print ad for the B&B in a major publication. Previously, she'd only advertised through small, classified-type ads in the back of magazines. The excitement only lasted a moment, though, when she realized she had no one to talk with about her new advertising plans.

It had been nearly two weeks since she'd talked with Matt and he hadn't returned either of Claire's two phone calls. She'd tried to tell herself he was busy, but in her heart she knew better.

Grabbing her car keys and her purse, Claire decided to have lunch at Matt's sister's little diner in town, hoping to find out what was going on with him.

"Just one," she said to the woman near the door, when she'd entered the small restaurant. '*My world of* **ones**' she thought to herself sliding into the booth.

Ordering a salad and cup of split pea soup, Claire casually asked the waitress, "Oh, by the way, doesn't Matt's sister own this restaurant?"

"Why, sure!" the older, freshly-permed waitress answered. "Do you know Matt?"

"Oh, ah, yes," Claire said. "He's done some work… I mean he's a friend, actually."

"Well!" the smiling woman said, "I'll let Annie know you're here! She'd want to say hello!"

Minutes later, a pretty, petite brunette in jeans and a blue floral blouse walked up.

"Claire!" she said, extending her hand, "I'm Annie!"

"So nice to meet you finally!" Claire said. "I've heard so much about you from Matt! Please, sit down, if you have time!"

Annie and Claire chatted for a few minutes while Claire waited for her food. "Thanks for sending over those crutches," Claire said. "They made a huge difference!"

"Oh, no problem!" Annie said, smiling. "Matt said he expected that you'd try to hobble around on that ankle, with or *without* crutches, so I thought I'd at least try to make it a bit easier for you!"

Taking a sip of her drink, Claire asked, "So, ss Matt okay? I haven't been able to reach him for a few days."

"Oh, sure! He's fine,' Annie said. "He's gone down into the valley on that big commercial job. Said it's easier to just stay local down there, rather than drive back and forth on the mountain."

Disappointed, Claire said, "Oh, I didn't know. He'd mentioned a big carpentry job, but…"

"Yeah!" Annie said. "That's the one!"

"Um," Claire went on casually, "Do you know when he's coming back?"

"Nope. No idea. You never know with my brother!" Annie answered. "He just asked me to look after his place. Said not to worry and that he'd be in touch."

When Claire's food arrived, she barely touched it. She realized she truly missed Matt and she wondered when, and *IF*, she'd see him again. Paying her check, Claire said good-bye to Annie and added, "Oh! If you should talk to Matt, would you let him know that I asked about him?"

Inside her SUV again, Claire leaned against the steering wheel, feeling alone and missing Matt. She closed her eyes, dreading that she had to drive home to her empty house.

Driving along the dirt road, back to her house, Claire had to pull to the side, to allow the oncoming mail truck to pass on the narrow road. As he passed by, the kindly old mailman waved and smiled. Unlike in the city, the mail carriers in the mountains drove their own vehicles when delivering the mail. Claire had grown accustomed every day to seeing the old green Jeep that delivered her mail.

Stopping at her mailbox, Claire found a huge envelope in her mailbox. Seeing the return address in the corner of the envelope, she realized it was another packet of mail that Elaine had collected at her Florida house and forwarded on to her.

'*This'll keep me busy*' she thought, happy to have a distraction for the afternoon.

Thumbing through all the envelopes and ads while sitting at her kitchen table, Claire sorted them into separate piles. Credit card bills; the lawn company; the pool service; investment statements; junk; junk and more junk.

Then, Claire came across a simple, tan-colored envelope. The return address listed a company called '***Donor Share.***' Assuming it was just another solicitation for a charitable contribution, or maybe an advertisement, Claire placed the envelope in the 'junk' pile and began opening her credit card statements.

An hour later, after writing checks to pay the bills she'd opened, Claire was feeling a bit antsy. Looking outside, she realized it would soon be dark.

The house was much too still. The silence was almost piercing. Claire wished she could phone Elaine, but she knew Elaine and Ryan were in the Bahamas for the week.

Grabbing her box of personalized stationery, Claire flipped the switch that turned on the lights in the gazebo outside, grabbed her blue plaid poncho from the wall hook beside the door and went to compose a good, old fashioned hand-written letter to her best friend.

If she 'couldn't phone Elaine, at least she could 'talk' to her in this way!' she thought to her self.

Dear El,

Bet you'll be surprised to have a letter from me when you get back! Hope you and Ryan had a great time and that you're both sporting perfect tans by now!

I wished I could have phoned you today. I really need to talk things through with someone. I think I've really made a mess of things up here.

You know how helpful Matt was to me when I sprained my ankle... Well, I tried to listen to your advice and 'give things a chance,' but I just didn't feel right. I'm not good at this! I'm so conflicted, El!

Like I told you before, Matt is such a great person. I've never met anyone like him before. Except for Daniel, that is. Matt is kind, considerate, intelligent, funny, and there's no denying that's he's gorgeous. WOW! I remember saying these exact same things to you when I'd met Daniel!

There's just something about Matt. Something so special and so comfortable feeling. And, if things were different... Well, who knows?

I just wish I knew what to do, El! I was so careful not to send him the wrong signals that I think I've alienated him now. I don't blame him. I guess he realized I'm a lost cause, because he's not returning any of my phone calls and he even took a job out of town. I don't even know if I'll see him again.

The kids met Matt, like I told you. Layne is supportive of my friendship with him, and Danny was starting to come around, but a little slower, to warm-up to Matt. Over-protective, just like his father!

I wish I knew what to do, El. I miss Daniel so much! But, I have to admit that I really enjoy being around Matt. It's so comfortable ~ so easy and natural feeling! Actually, Daniel and Matt are a lot alike in many ways. They'd have been friends, I'm sure. I just wish I had a sign or better yet ~ someone to simply tell me what to do! I'm so conflicted! I can't stand feeling like this much longer!

Anyhow, sorry to ramble! Give me a call when you've returned from globetrotting and we'll catch-up!

Hugs!
~ Claire

Licking the light blue envelope, Claire noticed the sun setting behind the treetops and creating shadows on the mountains in the distance. She pulled the poncho tighter around her shoulders and leaned against the lattice wall of the gazebo.

Watching the sun drop slowly, Claire saw a flock of birds flying over the treetops. One of the birds broke away and flew straight toward the gazebo, landing on a handrail only a few feet from Claire.

"Well, hello again, Little Guy," she said quietly, noticing the familiar small white patch on the chest of the tiny red bird. "You're becoming a regular visitor here, aren't you, buddy?"

A few days later, Claire was coming up her back steps, when she heard the phone ringing inside. Her heart beat faster, hearing the ring, and she rushed inside to grab it, just as it stopped ringing.

'*Got to get caller ID!*' she thought to herself. Not wanting to miss another call, Claire decided she'd finish weeding the garden another time, and she spent the rest of the day inside her house, just in case her phone rang again.

Claire spent much of her time just trying to busy herself and keep her mind occupied. She phoned the city licensing office in Florida, inquiring about what she needed to do to have her home licensed as a bed-and-breakfast. She inquired about zoning requirements. She phoned her insurance agent to ask about business liability coverage for the Florida B&B.

Claire knew *what* she needed to do in order to set-up her Florida business, but she somehow didn't feel as excited anymore about the new venture. She was glad she had more guests arriving at the mountain house in a few days. It would be a welcome distraction from constantly thinking of Matt.

Chapter 30

While her guests were in her home, Claire went about her business, being hospitable and friendly, providing huge homemade breakfasts and baked treats every afternoon. She chatted with Mr. and Mrs. Bell, enjoying having their company. But still, something was missing.

One afternoon, while shopping in town at the open-air farmer's market for fresh vegetables, Claire looked up to see a familiar red pick-up turning into the unpaved parking lot. Her heart beat faster, just seeing the truck.

Absent-mindedly, Claire ran a hand through her hair, adjusted her blouse and licked her lips, which she'd applied some lipstick to earlier.

Not wanting to seem anxious or excited to see Matt, she turned her back to the parking lot, her basket of vegetables hanging from her arm. She could actually *hear* her own heart beating now. She fumbled with an onion, keeping her back turned, aching to speak to Matt.

"Claire?" he said, "Is that you?" Relieved to hear his voice, Claire exhaled deeply.

"Oh! Matt!" she said, "I didn't see you come in!"

"Annie sent me over to pick-up an order for the diner," he said.

"Well I just stopped in for a few things, myself," Claire said, grinning. "So... Um... How've you been?"

"Good, good!" Matt said. "Just finished that big job I'd told you about."

"Oh, yeah," Claire said casually, "I met your sister and she told me about it."

There was an awkward silence, as both Claire and Matt stood only about two feet apart, smiling at one another, each searching desperately for something to say to bridge the uncomfortable silence.

Claire was sure that Matt could hear the thumping in her chest and she felt the heat rising up in her cheeks.

Finally, Matt said, "So how's business been for you lately?"

"Oh!" Claire said, "The B&B! Yes, I've had a few more guests. It's been good!"

"Well... It's uh..." Matt fumbled, "It's been really good seeing you, Claire. Really good."

The smile faded from Claire's face. "You, too," she said, not wanting Matt to leave.

"Well, take care," he said, turning to walk away, as Claire stood awkwardly still holding the onion in her hand.

"Uh, Matt," she called after him.

"Yeah?" he answered eagerly, spinning around.

"I'm doing a bonfire for my guests tonight. Would you like to stop by?" Claire asked hopefully.

"Gotta help Annie's husband move-in some new freezers at the diner tonight," Matt said, as Claire's disappointment became apparent to both of them.

"But I could come by later, if it's not too late," he quickly added.

"Oh, no!" Claire answered. "I mean… No, it won't be too late! Any time is good!"

"See you then," he said, grinning, and then he winked at Claire, before he turned to walk away.

When Claire got back to her house, the Bells were just pulling into the yard in their car too.

"Hi, there!" Claire said from the open window of her SUV.

"Hi, Claire," Mrs. Bell said. "Well, you two are back early from antiquing!" Claire said.

"Oh, we got a call that my sister is sick," Mrs. Bell said. "We need to be getting back right away."

"Oh, I'm so sorry," Claire said. "Are you leaving in the morning, then?"

"No, no," Mr. Bell answered from across the roof of his car, as he shut the car door. "We need to start heading back this evening, I think. Long drive, you know?"

An hour later, Claire was waving good-bye as the Bell's big sedan pulled away from her yard. Closing the kitchen door behind her, Claire leaned on it and wondered what Matt would think when he arrived later that night and found only Claire at the house, with no guests. She wondered if she should cancel with him, but she quickly decided against it. She really had missed him and was looking forward to seeing him again. She'd just explained that the Bells had left early for a family emergency.

Before dark could set in, Claire collected wood from the tree-lined area around the house. Wearing gardening gloves, she piled branches in the wheelbarrow, and then pushed it over to the fire pit.

Stacking the smallest branches first, she remembered how Daniel had taught her start a campfire for the first time, when they'd been camping in the Ocala National Forest.

Leaving the larger branches outside the fire pit, Claire then went inside to shower and freshen-up from her day.

She dressed in jeans and a pink, long sleeved v-neck T-shirt. She only put on a touch of make-up and pulled her long hair back into a ponytail, then twisted it up on her head and secured it with bobby pins, leaving just a few soft tendrils around her face.

Knowing Matt would arrive late that night, Claire decided to wait a while before starting the fire. She tried to busy herself around her house to pass the time. She removed the sheets from the Bell's bed, tidied their room and then did some laundry.

Looking at the wall clock in the kitchen, Claire saw it was only seven-thirty. The time seemed to be standing still, as she anticipated seeing Matt again.

Chapter 31

Sitting in a white, wooden Adirondack chair, tending the fire, Claire realized that she felt like a teenaged girl anxiously waiting for her date, both nervous and excited to see Matt. She tried to calm her nerves, leaning her head back against the tall chair her eyes. It was a perfect night with a clear, star-studded sky.

Finally, after what had seemed like hours, Claire heard the sound of tires on the rocky road leading to her house. Moments later, she saw headlights coming down the path, and she exhaled deeply with a sigh of relief, as she realized her heart was racing with excitement.

"Well, hey, there!" Matt said, stepping down and then closing the door of his truck. "Where *is* everybody?"

"Hey, yourself!" Claire said. "Well, the Bells had to go back early today. A family emergency, they said."

"Well, then, in that case..." he said, turning back toward his truck again.

Seconds later, Matt pulled a wine bottle from the cab of his truck. "I picked up a bottle of that wine we had at Catherine's restaurant a few months ago."

"Oh! How nice!" Claire said, getting up from her chair. "Let me get some glasses and a corkscrew from the kitchen!"

A few minutes later, Claire was back beside the fire. As Matt was uncorking the wine, he said, "You can build quite a fire!" Laughing, he added, "Were you a Girl Scout or something?"

"Oh, I've done it lots of times up here," Claire said, referring to the countless family trips that the Mitchells had taken to the mountain house.

After pouring two glasses of wine, Matt placed the bottle on a small wooden table beside one of the Adirondack chairs. Still standing, he held his glass up and toward Claire.

"To you, pretty lady," he said, watching the reflection of the flames dancing in Claire's eyes as the gentle breeze softly blew the loose tendrils of her hair toward her face.

"Thank you," Claire said, swallowing hard, as her heart raced even faster. Taking a sip, she said, "Here, you go. Sit down," indicating the nearby chair.

"You can't sit by a campfire in a *chair*," Matt joked, sitting down on the grass. "Here, sit on the ground, like a real camper!"

Claire was still standing, as Matt reached up and took her hand, pulling her gently toward the ground.

Laughing, she said, "Okay, you're probably right."

"Do that again," Matt said in a throaty voice.

"What?" Claire asked, puzzled.

"Laugh like that again," he answered, looking into her eyes as the flames warmed both of them. They both sat perfectly still, looking into each other's eyes, seeing more than just the reflection of the dancing flames.

Matt swallowed hard and then slowly he leaned toward Claire and gently kissed her lips. Closing her eyes, Claire relaxed and kissed Matt tenderly.

Leaning back, his heart racing, Matt said, "I hope that was okay."

"Uh, yes, I mean…" Claire stammered, "It was. Okay, I mean."

"I've wanted to do that for so long," Matt said, "It's hard for me to be around you sometimes Claire. I don't want to scare you away."

"I'm sorry," she said, squeezing her eyes shut, "I know I'm so complicated!"

"Well, 'Complicated' has never looked so beautiful to me," Matt said, leaning over to kiss Claire again.

Two hours later, as the fire was dying and smoldering, Matt and Claire still sat on the ground. Matt had insisted

Claire take the navy windbreaker he'd been wearing and he had wrapped an arm around Claire's shoulder, gently pulling her closer.

"You know," he went on, "I want you to know that I don't have any expectations at all, Claire. Just being near you is good enough for me. For now."

Feeling relaxed and realizing that she trusted Matt completely, she said, "I really missed you while you were gone, you know? It was pretty lonely out here without you."

Grinning, and obviously pleased, Matt pulled away a little, looking at her, and said, "You did?!"

Laughing, Claire pulled him toward her this time and kissed him, wrapping her arms around his broad shoulders.

"Yes! Very much!" she answered when she'd eventually released him. "And, I really have to admit something to you. I actually *saw* you pull in to the farmer's market!"

Now it was Matt who was laughing. "Well, I have to admit something, too! The only reason I turned in there was because I saw *your* SUV in the parking lot!"

And with that, they both were laughing, each genuinely pleased to find that the other one had pursued them.

"Should I put some more wood on the fire?" Matt asked, looking at the smoldering orange embers in the fire pit.

Disappointed to think that their evening might end, Claire said, "I don't even know what time it is!"

"Well, I don't have any place to be ~ do you?" Matt asked, reaching for more wood from the wheelbarrow beside the pit and tossing it on the fire, and then stoking the logs until the flames grew again.

As the two continued to easily talk, looking into the fire, Matt said, "So tell me all about what your family's like. I mean Danny and Layne. And even Dan."

Happy that Matt had invited her to talk about her kids and Daniel, Claire said, "Thank you."

"For what?" Matt asked, truly perplexed.

"For letting me know it's okay to talk about him."

"Claire, look," Matt began, as he looked into her eyes, "Your marriage to Dan is part of who you are… and I really *like* who you are. You can always talk to me. About anything."

"I believe that," she said, "I do."

After Claire had told Matt countless stories of the life she had shared with Daniel and her children, she told him of Daniel's illness and finally, of his death.

"You know," she went on, "I've never actually talked about it this much with anyone. Not even with Elaine."

"It must've been so hard for you," Matt said, "I can tell you two were really in love."

"Even though it ended too soon," Claire went on, "I wouldn't trade those years for anything."

"And I wouldn't want you to," Matt said, "Because it brought you here. Tonight. With me."

And he kissed her again, his warm mouth hungrily, yet tenderly caressing hers, inviting her to know him more.

Claire kissed him back, eagerly, as tears formed at the corners of her eyes.

"What is it?" Matt said, looking down at her.

"I never thought I'd feel it again," she answered, as Matt pulled her to his chest and held her.

She hugged him tight, comforted by the rhythmic beating of his heart as she inhaled his scent, feeling entirely safe and comfortable in his strong arms.

They sat silently by the fire, holding each other, but not saying a word. Finally, Matt said, "It's getting pretty cold out here now."

Looking at Matt in his denim shirt atop his red T-shirt, she said, "Oh! You must be freezing since you gave me your jacket! I'm sorry!"

"I was thinking about *you*," Matt said, laughing, "Your cheeks and hands are freezing."

"Yeah, we should go inside," Claire said, standing up and brushing off her jeans with her hands.

Matt grabbed a shovel from beside the fire pit and tossed dirt on the dying embers as Claire collected their wine glasses.

Inside the house, Claire said, "I didn't even offer you anything to eat tonight! Are you hungry?"

"I haven't thought about food for a second!" Matt laughed, closing the kitchen door behind him and stepping toward Claire. "I don't want to wear-out my welcome," he said, "Should I go?"

"Um, Ah, no," Claire answered, feeling a bit clumsy. Taking his hand and leading him to the living room, she said, "Let's go in here and warm-up a bit."

Claire removed Matt's windbreaker that she was still wearing and he took off his denim shirt and sat down on the sofa wearing just his T-shirt and jeans. They both slipped off their shoes.

Claire sat down beside Matt and curled her feet beneath herself on the sofa, leaning into him. Matt pulled her toward him, rubbing his hand on her arm to warm her. As they talked, Matt held her hand with his free hand, stroking her fingers as he listened to her.

They talked for another hour, and then they just sat quietly, as if they'd repeated the same scene for years. Claire soon fell asleep against Matt's chest, lulled to sleep by the comforting, rhythmic sound of his heartbeat.

With his arm wrapped around Claire, Matt fell asleep too, more content than he'd ever been before.

Hours later, as the sun shone brightly through the living room window, Claire squinted at the offending light, but she didn't dare to move. She leaned against Matt's chest, listening to his peaceful breathing, feeling the rise and fall of his chest against her.

Finally, when he stirred, Claire felt a bit disappointed. She'd been perfectly comfortable and she was certain that could have stayed in the same spot for the rest of day, nuzzled against Matt and tucked away from the rest of the world.

"Good morning," Claire said leaning back slightly and smiling, as Matt tried to stretch.

"Well, I've never opened my eyes to a more beautiful sight," Matt said. "But, I don't think your couch was made for sleeping!"

"I would have to agree!" Claire laughed, "And, boy, we both smell like a campfire, don't we?"

"Small price to pay for waking up with a beautiful woman in my arms!" Matt said, kissing Claire, "I'd do it again and again!"

Standing up, Claire said, "Well, if you don't mind giving me a minute to take a shower, I can make us some breakfast."

"Just don't go near those basement steps!" he joked.

"Very funny!" she answered, laughing too. "Hey," she added, "If you want to shower in the other bathroom, there's towels and a couple robes for guests on the back of the door. Might make you feel better!"

Minutes later, Claire was in her kitchen, wearing a thick, blue chenille robe, her hair wet and hanging loose on her shoulders. She was whisking eggs in a mixing bowl when Matt came into the kitchen. Coming up behind her, Matt wrapped his arms around Claire's waist. He squeezed her gently and kissed her neck through her wet hair, inhaling the sweet scent of her shampoo.

"I've decided that you *are* a complicated woman, Claire," he joked.

"I warned you!" she asked, turning to kiss his him. "But what exactly do you mean?"

"Well, I've been here all night. I woke up with you in my arms. You're making me breakfast. I'm standing in your kitchen, freshly showered and wearing a bathrobe. BUT…"

"But, you are a gentleman, apparently!" Claire joked.

"Not really," he said, turning Claire around to face him, "But, you're worth the wait." And he kissed her again.

After they'd eaten breakfast, Matt said, "I know I should probably go, but I really don't want to."

Claire stood up to take the empty plates from the table. "I don't want you to go either," she said, replacing the dishes back on the table.

Standing beside him, she ran her fingers through his wet hair. Matt encircled her waist and pulled her to him. She smelled like sweet soap and lilacs. Matt inhaled deeply, closing his eyes.

Claire looked down and kissed him passionately. He pulled her into his lap and hungrily kissed her, running his hand through her hair then inside the thick collar of her robe onto her soft shoulder.

"Claire," he said in a throaty, measured voice, "If you're not sure… I'm okay if…"

Pulling him toward her again, she said, "No, I'm sure."

Matt stood up, lifting Claire in his arms in one motion, as her robe slipped from her bare shoulder. He kissed her neck and then her shoulder as he carried her to her bedroom.

Forcing himself to be gentle with her, he laid Claire on her bed. As he untied the belt on her robe, Claire suddenly felt self-conscious. She put her hand on his, "Matt, I… I… There's been no one else for me but Daniel."

Kissing her again, he said, "I'll try not to disappoint then! Be patient with me!"

Relieved by his humor, Claire kissed him again, allowing him to open her robe. She reached for the tie on his robe, pulling him to her. He gently laid atop her, careful not to fully put his weight on her. They both moaned appreciatively as their warm flesh touched.

Running her hands over his muscular shoulders and down his back, Claire opened her eyes own to look into Matt's as he looked down at her. They both felt an connection, almost as if they'd been together for years.

"You make me so comfortable. I feel like I've known you forever. Is it… Can it be possible that I love you?" she asked, already knowing the answer.

"I really hope so," he said, looking deeply into her eyes, "Because I've known for a while that I love you, Claire."

Claire looked down, at Matt's chest. Realizing that she was looking at his chest, Matt swallowed hard, feeling uncomfortable and a bit embarrassed.

"What?" she started, quizzically looking at his muscular chest. "What happened?"

"That's the long story that I'd mentioned before," he said. "But, do you think can we talk about it later?"

Claire kissed the long scar that ran the entire length of Matt's chest and down toward his tight, muscular abdomen.

Hours later, as Claire lay in Matt's arms, under the quilt on her bed, she said, "I really think I could get used to this."

Smiling, Matt kissed the top of her head. "I don't know if I've ever felt so happy, Claire."

Running her fingers down the long scar on Matt's otherwise perfect chest, she asked, "Will you tell me about this now?"

Matt explained that he'd had a congenital heart condition that was diagnosed when he was in college. "It got progressively worse and worse," he explained. "I was exhausted all time. Couldn't catch my breath. It was miserable. I had to stop working out, obviously, but the doctors said I lasted as long as I did because I was in otherwise great shape."

Claire listened quietly, looking into Matt's eyes, her heart breaking for him because he'd been through so much.

"I ended the relationship I'd be in because I couldn't put her through all that," he said. "Thank God for my sister! Annie had to take care of me for a while, which I know was a burden to her. She has a husband and kids, and the restaurant, you know. I moved up here, to the mountains, so she could at least still care for her family while she was also helping me."

"And than, finally, I was put on a donor list for a transplant. Then, all of a sudden, out of the blue, we got the call that they'd found a match for me. It all went very fast from that point."

Claire hugged him close as he continued.

"So, a few months ago," he went on, "When I met you, I was just so thankful to still be alive and to have met you. Just to have *known* you, Claire! I knew that I was blessed to be alive!"

With tears in her eyes, Claire continued to listen quietly to all he'd been through.

"After I met you, it became even more important to me to thank the family that so selflessly had given me the heart of their loved one. It had always bothered me that someone else had to die, so I could live. You can't imagine how emotional it was for me. So, my sister suggested that I call my heart surgeon's office and then they put me in touch with an organization called ***Donor Share***."

'Oh my….' Claire thought to herself, her own heart racing, as she remembered the tan envelope that she'd never opened, assuming it was simply junk mail.

"Well," Matt went on, "So, I told them that I just wanted to thank the donor's family. But they said there were all kinds of rules and privacy issues, but they'd still give it a shot and would try to make contact for me."

Claire nodded, encouraging Matt to continue, and then she laid her head on his chest and closed her eyes, listening to his heartbeat, as he went on.

"Apparently," Matt continued, "*Donor Share* sent a request to the donor's family, asking if we could meet. But, they still haven't had a response from the family. I realize that it might be hard for them to meet the recipient, so it may never happen. But, now that I'm so in love with you, Claire, I *especially* want them to know that I'll *always* be so grateful for the new life they gave me. **Always.**"

Claire kissed Matt again, tears filling her eyes. She kissed his chest, and then kissed his mouth again fully and passionately, with tears streaming down her cheeks and onto her bare breasts as she held him tightly.

"It's okay now," Matt said, surprised at Claire's intense reaction to his story. Stroking her hair, he said, "I'm fine now. Really. I'm just so grateful to be here with you! I want to be with you *always*,

Claire! An entire *lifetime* with you could never be enough!"

Claire held him tighter, knowing that it was **she** who was actually the grateful one.

"*Forever and always,*" she whispered, as the little, red bird flew past the bedroom window and soared high above the mountaintops in the distance.

■■■

Weeks later, Matt and Claire stood, arms wrapped around one another, watching as the new, heart-shaped sign for her bed-and-breakfast was finally erected by the main highway.

'*Forever & Always B&B*' it read.

* * * * * *